D1084469

Desilicious

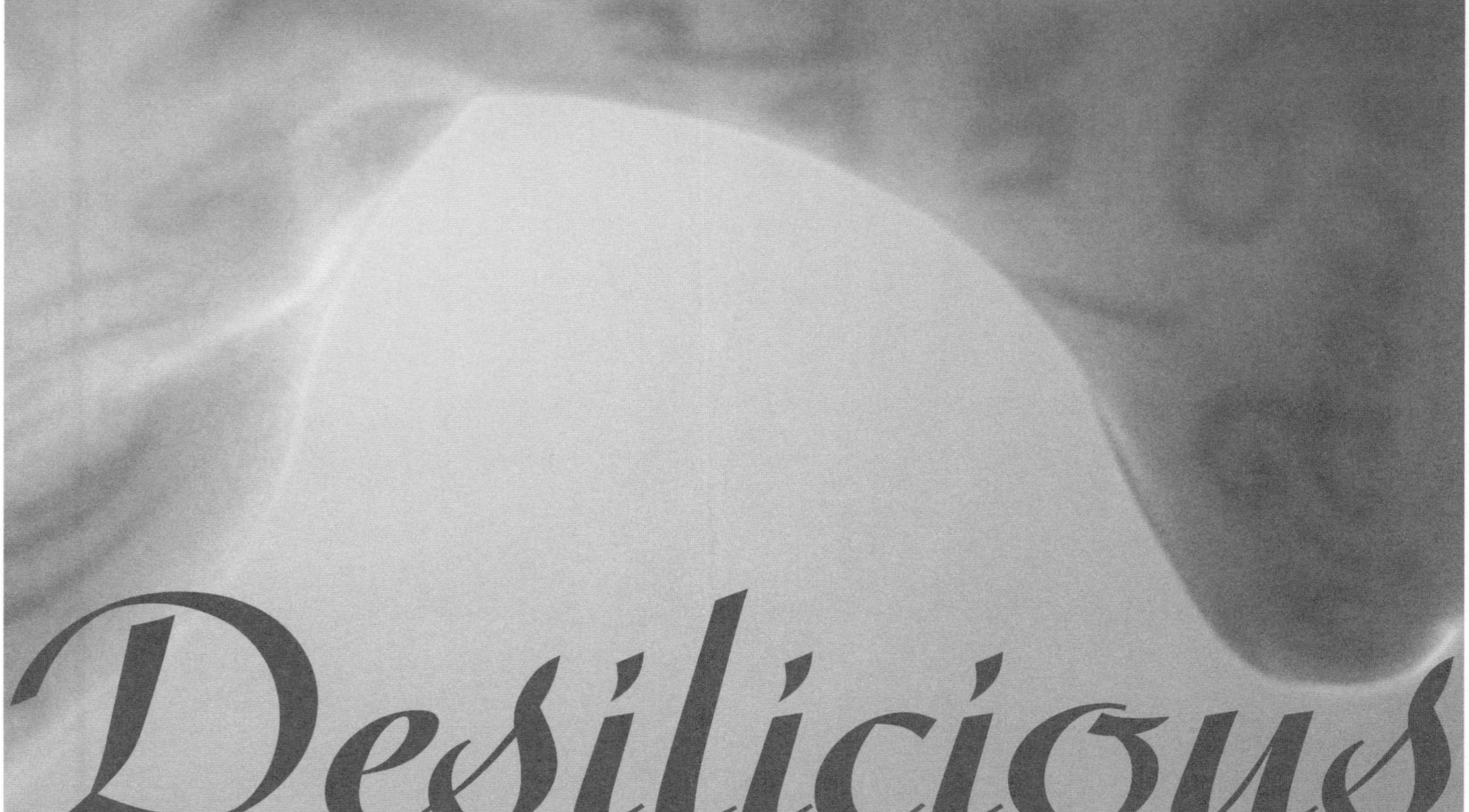
Desilicious

808.
3085
DES

Sexy.

Subversive.

South Asian.

EDITED BY THE
MASALA TROIS COLLECTIVE

FINKELSTEIN
MEMORIAL LIBRARY
SPRING VALLEY, N.Y.

ARSENAL
PULP PRESS
Vancouver

3 2191 00764 1862

DESILICIOUS: SEXY. SUBVERSIVE. SOUTH ASIAN.
Stories copyright © 2003 by the authors, unless otherwise indicated
Introduction copyright © 2003 by the editors

All rights reserved. No part of this book may be reproduced or used in any form by
any means – graphic, electronic or mechanical – without the prior written permission
of the publisher, except by a reviewer, who may use brief excerpts in a review,
or in the case of photocopying in Canada, a license from Access Copyright.

ARSENAL PULP PRESS
103 - 1014 Homer Street
Vancouver, B.C.
Canada V6B 2W9
arsenalpulp.com

The publisher gratefully acknowledges the support of the
Canada Council for the Arts and the British Columbia Arts Council for
its publishing program, and the Government of Canada through the
Book Publishing Industry Development Program for its publishing activities.

Design by Solo
Cover photography by Heather Dubbeldam from Script II series, 2001

Printed and bound in Canada

This is a work of fiction. Any resemblance of characters to persons
either living or deceased is purely coincidental.

National Library of Canada
Cataloguing in Publication Data

Main entry under title:
Desilicious : Sexy. Subversive. South Asian. / Masala Trois Collective.

ISBN 1-55152-154-7

1. Erotic stories, South Asian. I. Masala Trois Collective.

PN6120.95.E7D47 2003   808.83'93538   C2003-911203-9

Contents

Sex is not something we do, it is something we are.
– Mary Calderone, from *Human Sexual Experience*

Sex is hardly ever just about sex.
– Shirley MacLaine

Acknowledgments

The Masala Trois Collective would like to thank the talented team of volunteers who helped spread the word about *Desilicious*. Tanveer Bookwala, Meharoona Ghani, Rahil Khan, Zainab Moghul, Ruby Nagpal, Priti Patel, Nisha Sajnani, Beesham Seecharan, Soniya Sheth, Rachpal Sidhu Grewal, Anoop Singh – thank you for your time and enthusiastic support.

Many thanks also go out to our extended team. Pamela Arora, Raj Bhanot, Ann Decter, Terry Guerriero, James Ip, Kamal Mundi, Vick Naresh, Lata Wadhwani – we greatly appreciate your expert advice and your skills, but most of all for putting up with all our questions and requests!

Jag Gundu – thanks for making us look good! Heather Dubbledam – we couldn't have dreamed of a better image for our cover! And a warm thank you to the South Asian Professionals' Networking Association for their encouragement and support.

Brian Lam, Blaine Kyllo, Kiran Gill Judge – our wonderful new friends at Arsenal Pulp Press – thank you for your patience, your guidance, and most of all for your belief in this project.

Finally, we want to thank our family and friends for braving the *gup-shup* circulating among extended family and community members about "those kids and that sex book." We heard the snickers from *those* uncles, and saw the raised eyebrows from *those* aunties, but the nudges and winks we received from our grandmothers assured us that those very aunties and uncles would be the first ones picking up this book.

Foreplay

Desilicious presents sexuality and culture as inseparable forces. Sex shapes culture, and culture shapes sex. In these stories, poems, and personal essays, sexuality and culture blend and burn into each other, deeply. Fantasies flirt with memories, and secret desires tease public denials. Each selection uniquely tailors the language of the libido to adorn and, ultimately, uncover symbolic liaisons between South Asian cultures and sexualities.

And these liaisons, of course, are as ancient as they are alive. Even a cursory survey of historical and contemporary South Asian art, dance, fashion, music, film, and literature critically affirms the sexual ardour – and tensions – that lace South Asian cultures.

Engaging the richness and complexity of sexuality in South Asian cultures, however, can be an entangling affair. Numerous crude caricatures and sexist stereotypes of South Asian sexualities linger stubbornly in our postcolonial zeitgeist: South Asians continue to be represented frequently either as repressed victims of sexless arranged marriages, or as hypersexual inheritors of the *Kama Sutra*. Selections in *Desilicious* subversively sample and remix several "familiar" narratives of South Asian sexuality, creatively exploring a range of desires thriving between these polarized stereotypes.

Some of these explorations are romantic, others risqué. Several *Desilicious* writers offer meditations on sensuality as a medium of cultural exchange. Others make compelling cases for the intense sexiness of modesty. Some confront the mysterious power of inhibitions. Many revel in sexual discovery, especially as it impassions self-discovery. Others struggle with sexual denial as if it were a stubborn, childproof bottle of Ayurvedic aphrodisiacs. *Desilicious*, over all, challenges and expands assumptions about what is "erotic." Selections in *Desilicious* remind us that eroticism surrounds us, that sensuality engages *all* our senses. Geography, weather, voices, fabrics, and foods – to name only a few tropes – are given more attention in *Desilicious* than explicit descriptions of genital friction or ticklish erogenous zones. From tender to torrid, selections offer a range of reflections on the sensuality of the "everyday." Beyond candle-lit dinners and beds smothered with roses, contributors to *Desilicious* engage the longing for consummation nascent in each of our senses.

We formed the Masala Trois collective casually, over coffee during a cold, dark, bone-chilling autumn evening in Toronto, one that predictably pushes imaginations to warmer thoughts. Our brand of "proper desi upbringing" inhibited us from asking, straight up, "Getting any?" So, being fellow lovers of literature, someone asked the next most obvious question: "It's been a while since I read any sexually-themed South Asian work . . . anyone know of any titles?" After recounting some of our favourites, we began wondering why so many wonderful stories about brown folks getting down – stories we had heard, experienced, or dreamt about – were so difficult to find.

And so the three of us, sitting in some generic Second Cup, talking loudly about sex, *sans* shame, wondered how we could give readers a generous dose of much needed desi lovin' – in all its tenderness, wonder, surprise, and, yes, even messed-up-ness. We never had any grand ambitions of representing the entire diversity of South Asian sexual experience (could any volume?). At best, we hoped *Desilicious* could spark a much larger exploration of South Asian sexualities – *especially* those modes of sexual being and sensual living that extend beyond the borders of this collection.

Yes, we did receive stern (and, ironically, similarly worded) critiques from "traditionalists" and "progressives." People of all types, it seems, can have aversions to getting turned on. We endured uncomfortable grins from family members at dinner parties, wondered (secretly, so secretly) whether the book would add or detract from our eligibility. And though friends were generally supportive, some felt compelled to share concerns: "How are you going to feel about your son reading this in a few years?" "Do you think this is going to scare away potential in-laws?" and, "If you really want to hook up, why not just crash the wedding circuit next summer instead of doing *all this work?*"

By far, however, the feedback we received was tremendously positive; we were encouraged throughout the project. Beyond the hundreds of submissions we received, many sent simple notes, saying, "It's about time!" And that, for us, is enough.

Desilicious is, ultimately, a collection of steamy, saucy, sexy desi writing. Desi – derived from the Hindi word for homeland, *desh* – is to "South Asian" what *black* is to "African American" or *Chicano* is to "Latino." Desi is a chameleon-like word, evocative more than descriptive, adopted most comfortably by young South Asians who appreciate the irony of naming a mind-bogglingly diverse number of cultural communities, spread across continents, using a word that simply suggests *home*. Desi is a word steeped in thick irony, for even as *Desilicious* begins mapping trajectories of desi desire, it slowly reveals how borders between the provinces of sexuality, memory, culture, and fantasy are constantly fading, blurring, and being recast.

– The Masala Trois Collective
  (Deborah Barretto, Gurbir Singh Jolly, Zenia Wadhwani)

Black Cumin

SHOMPABALLI DATTA

Black cumin
nazuk in hot oil
twirls up a delicate fragrance
and can't hardly wait
for bangled hands
cupping freshly diced vegetables
to stop its burning

Green Mango Sap

SHOMPABALLI DATTA

Kaalbaishakhi
and mangoes showered
faster than we could gather
in little hands

Some had fallen
still carrying the stalk
some ripped
scarred

Too many at once
we held them close
shirts stained and sticky
with sap

The sharp smell lingers
like love on my fingers
as I remember
green mango sap

Tiger, Tiger

TANUJA DESAI HIDIER

In the bar where she waits, the air is thick with smoke and men's voices. It is difficult to breathe. A jukebox stabs a beat through the fog; she does not know the song, but it reminds her of others, the ones where she can guess the ends of verses: blue is followed by true, cry by lie, and women love only men in a rhyming universe.

She drinks a zombie, bangles sparking against her wrist. Tristan wasn't in section today. It was the last time she was assistant-teaching before exams for Professor Bergman's Literature and the City course. She led a discussion on *Invisible Cities*, her peers' lively debate smoothing over her frequent moments of distraction. For just over two weeks, she and Tristan had been walking together after section to his apartment down the hill. Today, she walked alone and, when she buzzed the building two doors beyond the bar, discovered he wasn't home either. She was about to return to her place on Hope, but then decided to give him just five more minutes, and went into the bar where she'd be safe and could down a drink or two. Tonight, she thinks, picking at the chain around her neck, she will tell him. First she will apologize for her behaviour last night, but will go on to announce, calmly and firmly, that it must be over now, whatever it is they've been engaged in recently, or, at any rate, not continued after this evening unless he could accept not sleeping with her, and maybe not even then. Alternatively, if she lost her nerve, she would at the very least be pointedly vague about their next meeting. She would not add that experience had taught her that this – two weeks – was just about the length of time her near-lovers could tolerate her ultimate refusal, a celibacy she'd been clinging to with a confused fervour ever since the only time she'd let it go: two years before with the one who'd been her own teaching assistant, in the spring, in Paris.

Around her neck is a tiger nail on a gold chain. She fidgets with it between bitten-down fingernails. Her uncle Ramesh killed the tiger in the jungle outside of Bombay when her mother Shashikala was a girl. He and his friend heard its approach while hunting and scrambled, terrified, up a nearby tree. Night rushed down on them and in the tree they crouched, her uncle shooting blindly into the darkness, afraid to move. Like this they passed a sleepless night. Hours later, the tiger's haunches rolled up out of the green mist; it was shot seven times through. The boys, fearful that as soon as they descended the creature would leap for their hearts, shot again to be sure, and so the fur was rendered worthless. Later, however, a bit of the meat was cooked, and Ramesh's friends met to swallow the minimum amount required for eternal protection from illness and harm. Shashikala had been too sickened to eat any, and had made her realm of jurisdiction the tiger claws, which were pried off the dead beast and sunk in gold. The girl was generous to a fault, though, and the claws vanished quickly into the hands of suddenly solicitous cousins and curious children, a mendicant, astrologer, and local tea vendor who stood in a notched sea of smashed cow-dung cups and fixed his mesmerizingly small-pupiled eyes upon her till only one remained: the one linked around his mother's neck by Ramesh himself. This was the nail that had been saved, guarded ferociously by Ramesh and Shashikala's parents for the grandchild they longed for one day.

Kayla's uncle used to frighten her mother by telling her if she swallowed sweet lime seeds, trees would take root in her stomach and eventually thrust their laden branches from her mouth. However, when anyone else had tried to tease his precious *bacchoodi*, he'd grown infuriated, his nostrils flaring to surprising dimensions. He would chase the miscreants with sticks straight into Powai Lake, shouting out *Bhainchod!* and *Chutia!* and *Matherchot!*, the finest profanities he could muster. These words Kayla's mother did not understand then, and to this day expressed only with a noiseless mouthing of the first syllables. *Bhain*, she'd whisper, her cheek dimpling, *Chu. Mather.* Sisterfucker, buttfucker, motherfucker – the translations to English seem so impersonal, so tepid, Kayla thinks, all singularity quelled by their measured strut.

Ramesh had been slim and brown as a pencil, with fleshy eyelids. His cowlicks had splayed his hair awkwardly on both sides. Kayla saw his pictures in the family albums, in which he seems to be concentrating very hard on something just past the camera, his body always pressed close to a knickered, grinning Shashikala she could hardly recognize. He was killed in a motorcycle crash a few years after the tiger incident.

With the tiny pink umbrella, she stirs the ice melting at the glass bottom. She thinks of Tristan's face, and back a few semesters to Patrick's and Treat's: boy faces with appled cheeks and mothlike gazes. In India, her mother and father's was an unfluttering courtship, without kisses, without caresses. Later – after they'd circled each other, draped in hyacinth and rose, for the seven steps of the marriage ceremony – they were each other's first and only lovers. They'd slept together at least once – Kayla was satisfied she was proof of that when pubescence punctuated her body just like her mother's – but she is not convinced their nuptial frolics ever exceeded this number. The two seem more like siblings to her than husband and wife, even like mother and son, and with that came the powerful sense that their relationship could not be destroyed.

She can catch her mother's ancient life in strands, like music pouring from the window of a passing train. This song is one she knows she will always hear only from a distance, a thought that is both an ache and a relief. Tristan's flushed features and broad-cut body disorient her just as much as her mother's conversations with aunts and older cousins in Marathi, the language Kayla lost over the years in America. Her mother's words pressed forth, moist and sparkly as a pomegranate breaking open; when she spoke, Kayla plunged into a memory of herself as a baby, sitting naked on the cement floor in Bombay, rubbing blurry pink mango peels all over her body. Marathi, though now incomprehensible to her, warms her in a way that English with its corners and clearly delineated spaces has never been able to.

– I'm interested in a monogamous sexual relationship, Tristan told her two nights before. – Just you. No one else. You see, there is no need to use a condom.

She glances around the bar. Though she knows no one, the faces are familiar. Lighters flick on a world of narrowed eyes and the grizzled upper lips of men, inhaling with accustomed desperation from hand-rolled cigarettes. She nods for the bill, thinking of how Tristan's kisses leave her breathless, how his desire in much the same way wicks the life from her. His is a steel embrace, as if he is saying, *Don't worry, I will keep it all under control if you just hold perfectly still.* He is painfully observant; Kayla saw how his eyes flickered across rooms and streets, bars and bleachers, landing with a flattering intensity upon the found female element, the same way they rested on her for weeks in the student lounge where section was held.

All semester she felt the yellowish vortex of his eyes as she sat cross-legged on the lounge floor. She quoted Rilke, analyzed Strindberg, all the time made physically aware of her body by his gaze: its nakedness marked by the warm patches on her buttocks, slow pull of inner thighs, the quiet push of her nipples against silk, and the trickle of gold cool around her neck. Her hair was long, black as a bull's flank, to her hips. She used it to hide the eye that told too much, the corner of mouth that smiled when it shouldn't, shielded her profile when it seemed, as it often did, foreign and stark. She felt she had the head of an alien, with its wide forehead and eyes, and the unyielding jut of skull behind her ears. Hats did not fit her. Tristan was always watching her.

This was the same class that was assistant-taught two years previously by – as she, a freshman then, believed – an astonishingly erudite upperclassman who was, later, during a year abroad, quite pleased to initiate the eager ex-student into his kingdom of fleeting light. He did this late one evening in a park in the ninth *arrondisement* in Paris; her back arched and ground against the pebbles, damp with April, as the space between her legs widened and ached for the first time.

– Move that goddamned necklace, it's poking me, he'd muttered, sliding the tiger nail round to the back of her neck. Its tiny dig there comforted her, distracted her from the sensation that her entire body was turning porous, and she floating above it, waiting for the shifting below to cease, for it to be safe to come down again.

He laid his hand over her mouth and stifled a gasp just as an elderly couple passed nearby, leaning on each other for support.

– You must be built wrong, he told her after. – Or you would have enjoyed it.

~

In India, where she'd been until the age of five, Kayla had been the fat one, her cousins and aunts all a scant ninety pounds or under, their torsos stemming diaphanously up from wide-wound pelvises. She'd been the loud one, too; she broke into wild peals of laughter in temples and monasteries – once even at a cremation, so delighted had she been at the idea of one's body cindering down and scattering, vanishing completely. She'd been asked to lower her voice, gather her *chapphals* from the rambling mass by the threshold, and wait outside.

She leaves a dollar under the empty glass and leaps from the stool. She can feel the hot flare of men's eyes trailing her as she leaves. Unfortunately, down this part of the hill, there was no other place for her to wait. The days are getting dark as soon as they get light and it is a dangerous thing, especially lately, for a woman to walk alone through parts of the campus. Three weeks before, a freshman had been attacked in a parking lot at five o'clock in the afternoon, dusk still in her eyes; a week prior to that, a graduate student living off campus had been assaulted repeatedly by two men who tore her door right off its hinges. Rape whistles were handed out in the post office and women's centre, and at the roadside stands set up by the yellow-jacketed students of the university's sexual harassment patrol.

Wrapping herself in her arms, she walks down toward Tristan's building, taking hurried steps through the leaves on the ground. She thinks of the whistles, quickens her pace. They are striped red and yellow, with emergency numbers stamped on in black. She doesn't have one, but then she doesn't usually wander around alone after dark, nor talk to strangers, make eye contact, or engage in otherwise dangerous activities. Her mother, who is from the warrior caste, *Kshatriya*, and knows these things, had always told her the tiger nail would protect her and that fate only worked in retrospect.

She thinks backward towards her fate. Her thoughts glow from the rum. She gropes at them, tries to separate and order them into a logical path. She can see how the whole affair started, but is still struck by how immediately she – the charmer, the teacher – lost her footing as soon as it slipped from class to bedroom. For her it is over now, as there is nothing left for them to do but sleep together, which seems like a bad reason to do so (though, she fears, not enough of a reason not to). But she does not know how to begin to say no, when it is she who has brought them, yes by yes, to this point in the first place: in her moaning desire to tide out of herself into his hands, in her saying nothing at all, even in the way she taught class.

She remembers the section on Miller's *Tropic of Cancer*, how she blinked slowly, allowed herself to say it:

– The cunt is integral to Miller's conception of female sexuality.

The voice speaking did not sound like hers. No one said anything. She felt her hand slide up between her breasts to hold the gold-tipped pendant there. Her heart beat heavily against her palm, as if it were the only thing inside her; it had beaten between her legs when she said it, where the seam of her pants tingled. Tristan was very still, watching her. She did not turn away, and had the intoxicating sensation, for the first time, that her eyes had their own vortex, that *she* was pulling him into *her* world, that for the first time the other was coming to *her*.

He approached her after the rest of the students left.

– I just had to tell you, he said. – You have taught me so much. You've taught me to see the world in a whole new way. You are so different from anything I've ever experienced. I mean, your class is.

– I'm really happy to hear that, she said, and in the emptied room, was shy and looked down, pretending to search for something in her papers.

– I'm really happy, too, said Tristan. – To be here.

She didn't know what to say. Her stomach, as if to collapse the silence, groaned. She let her hair fall forward.

– I just had a great idea, he said. – Do you want to grab some Indian food? We could stuff ourselves, talk a little Miller. That is, if you're not afraid to be seen with a student.

She lifted her face, remembered she was the teacher.

– I'm not afraid, she said.

In the restaurant, he asked her to order. They had chicken *tikka masala* and *naan* thick with *jaggery*, and King Fisher beer. He wanted her to correct him, spell words, pronounce slowly. He fixed his eyes on her mouth as it funnelled sound for him. He told her – as she tore the bread and smeared it with mango jam – that he found eating with the hands not only sensible, but much more sensual. Outside, it grew dark while they lingered, not discussing literature.

– I love Indian food, he said. – It's so hot and exotic, so colourful.

He seized the bill from the waiter's hand, and put his finger to her lips when she protested.

– Like Indian women, he said. – Like you.

He walked her to her door, insisting that it just wasn't safe around town for a girl lookin' like she did. They stood under the ginkgo tree, suffused with a pale gold light even at that hour. He reached up to snap a silken leaf from a lower bough, and handed it to her.

– You've shown me so much, he said. – I want you to keep showing me things.

They stared at each other a long time. She twisted her chain. His face neared, dissolved, and they kissed, tasting of fennel and cumin and beer.

She went inside, but seconds later there was a tap at the door. When she opened it, Tristan was there, swaying. He reached out and pressed something into her hand.

– You must have dropped this, he said. – When we were . . . you know.

The tiger nail coiled up warm in her palm. She was sleepy and tipsy. The sight of it filled her with nostalgia and she wanted so much to love him.

– Come in, she said. – Don't go yet.

– I want to come in, Teacher, he said. – More than anything.

She glows, her edges softened, the drink pooled down. She can't feel the weather. She points the tiger nail into her palm, barely slitting the numbness. At Tristan's door, she holds her hand at the buzzer and is surprised at the crimson valley the claw has imprinted there.

– Hey, Kayla, come on up, his voice jets out of the little holes, narrow and distant, as if from the bottom of a well. – I just got in.

She walks up the two flights, very slowly. On the landing before his door, she hesitates.

Tristan's apartment is a one-bedroom set up for two people via a convertible sofa, but his roommate spends every other night at the dorm of his girlfriend, a Liverpudlian with blonde hair to her hips, Cleopatra bangs, eyes smudged to the ducts with makeup, and a nose-ring. The night before, Sly and Eve were there when Kayla arrived, Sly sucking on an apple bong and exhaling into Eve's mouth, his tongue uncoiling the smoke down her open throat. Eve was in Sly's lap, her skirt hiked up just past her underwear, and Sly's hand slithered under its hem. He clinched her there when he held the smoke in, his eyes tightly shut.

Though they were only feet from the door, neither seemed to notice Kayla's arrival. She sat next to Tristan on the pullout bed where he was lying, eyes bloodshot, cigarette silvering between his fingers. He hoisted himself up and thrust his feet into the slippers he kept by the bed to couch his night-time stumbles to the bathroom; he had cold feet, with curled-over toenails that left Kayla's shins scratched. He leaned in to kiss her, and she was just about to ask where they should go when his tongue flicked against her teeth, and she felt his hand sliding up between her legs. She could see Sly and Eve watching then, unblinkingly, from the couch. Sly's fingers jerked around more quickly under Eve's skirt.

– I can't, Kayla whispered, tearing her head back. – What are you doing? Not with them here.

– Oh, don't worry, Teacher, Tristan slurred. – We're in our own world. Us and them, we're parallel universes.

He began to mimic Sly's gestures on the crotch of her jeans.

– You'll get used to it, he said.

She longed to see it his way, to melt under the pressure of his fingers as her own hands had taught her she could – so many years ago, in the sun patch of her young bedroom – but she could not shake the feeling that, in this room where everybody was doing the same thing and no one was hiding, she was the only one revealed.

– I don't get used to anything. She nearly sobbed when she said it, and stood, swinging up her knapsack. – I can't and I don't.

– Whoa, freaking so soon? Tristan smiled and flopped back on the bed. – What a sweet little baby you are. Your big brown eyes and your big bad morals.

– If it were a question of morals, she began. At least then, she thought, she could do either the right thing or wrong, launch herself out of this grey area she so often inhabited.

But she didn't have the energy to justify herself, and said nothing. As she slipped into the hall, Tristan's laughter, mixed with the machinist clatter of Eve and Sly's dark chortles, chased after her down the stairs and into the street, mingling then with the voices, dulled through window panes, of the men in the bar next door.

On the landing, she runs a hand through her hair. Then knocks, tries the knob. It is unlocked and she goes in.

– Hi, she says, closing the door behind her. Her eyes adjust to the drop in light.

Tristan is slumped on the pull-out bed, his face patterned by the twirling Chinese lantern. Lids drifting, lips slippery. His fingers choke the neck of a tequila bottle.

– Hey there, he says. – Come closer, stranger.

She tries to imagine him as he was in class. In her mind, she assembles behind him first the high walls then the windows of the student lounge, slaps him back against a wooden chair and pretends he is watching her break down Robbe-Grillet, rather than fumbling towards him, bent on proving her ability to nimbly blend into his undulating world. It is not so difficult to imagine that other room. She sees now that the boy before her today was the boy in the lounge all along. The coincidence is startling, as she feels so far from the young woman she was in that other place.

– You weren't in class today. It was the last one.

– I had to see a friend, he says. Light spins over his eyes, turns them transparent. – How was it? A grand finale?

She doesn't know where he's been. His radio is playing that song, *Maybe if you would be true, darling I wouldn't be so blue*.

– Yeah, it was good, she says. – Amazing, actually, yes. And, well, about the way I acted last night, I just want to say –

– Aw, don't sweat it, Teacher, he says, and a smile wags across his face. – We have time to remedy that yet.

He stares at her a long time.

– You look beautiful in this light, he says. –Like a tiger.

– That's funny, she says, her shoulders unhunching a little. – I've got a tiger nail around my neck. My uncle killed it in the jungle in Maharashtra.

– Shh, he says. – Hold still. You are so beautiful when you hold still. Let the light pass over you.

She imagines the outline of a hand against her mouth and holds back a cry of indignation. After Ramesh was killed, her mother had told her once, no one would ever again say his name in that house in Bombay; instead, they passed the days in a slow silence, as if underwater, carefully numbing themselves against each other.

She focuses on the way the tequila is lit up, a melt of garnets and rubies like the ones the British swiped from the Taj Mahal. The jeweled glass nears her. Grateful, she takes the bottle, tilting to her mouth the slow burn; it radiates out, merges with the haze already enveloping her. The bottle rises like a bugle as she drains it, the glass paling a shade.

– That's some swallow you've got there, says Tristan, taking the bottle back with one hand and setting it on the bedside crate; with the other, he loops into her belt hook and pulls her closer.

– You've got a leaf in your hair, he says, and like the magician at a hazy birthday party, draws a delicate yellow ginkgo fan from behind her ear. It looks inappropriate in this room. – You heathen tiger child. I'll bet you fuck like a tiger too.

– But I can't, she blurts. Blurting is exhausting. Her voice sounds like it does on tape, heightened and as if in another room. – I won't. Remember. I wanted to talk to you about that.

– Queen of the *Kama Sutra*, he says. – You are too modest. Your people wrote the book of love. I'll bet you know all sorts of tricks. I've seen the paintings.

– I'm not so flexible, she says. – And no one in India does that stuff, anyway. It's all hype.

– You've got leaves all over you, he says, and pulls the twisted chain and then the flesh of her neck between his teeth. – Lie down. Let me brush you off.

~

In Paris, that April, that evening, she and the teaching assistant had gotten up, brushed the twigs and pebbles from their clothes, and walked back to his apartment on *rue* Perdue. It wasn't really a street but an underground walkway, with elevators creaking up to the thirteenth-floor apartment he shared with his half-brother and half-brother's girlfriend, an enthusiastic, moaning woman who, later that week, alarmed by the lack of parallel moaning on the wall's other side, offered to advise Kayla on how to position herself for *le plaisir maximum*.

That night, after, the teaching assistant had taken Kayla home by a roundabout route. He pointed out where and how Baudelaire had rhymed, Proust remembered, Nietzsche recurred – the information that had drawn her to him in the first place. Then, just as hope was reinstalling itself in her frazzled nerves, he proceeded to tick off a list of all the people he'd ever slept with: mostly women, prostitutes, *au pairs*, bartenders, students, peers, a professor, more students, friends' lovers and ex-lovers, once a chum's mother, sunbathers in Ibiza, swimmers in Crete, painters with spattered hands and a language of unknown origin in the Basque country, and, just days before, his half-brother's girlfriend.

Desilicious

– That's my list, he said, grinning. They were standing on *rue* Touillier, below the apartment in which Rilke had lived. The window was open and a breeze creaked its hinges. – Now it's your turn.

She said nothing, sought frantically in her head for lines from Rilke to guide her, but could only come up with the first words of the *Notebooks of Malte Laurids Brigge*:

So this is where people come to live; I would have thought it is a city to die in.

– *Me!* he answered jubilantly for her. – That was easy.

– A city to die in, she said. Looking up at the window, she could see a light on somewhere inside; a soft thud of footsteps, and then a child's hand reached into the faded day to pull in the window and lock it. She was dazzled with loneliness.

– You're my fourth virgin, he said solemnly.

Later, he gripped her head and pulled her down to his groin, groaning and sputtering; by the end of the week, he told her with a mother's pride that she would make a fine lover, and perhaps teacher – was there a difference? weren't both about kindling desire? – to many men and perhaps women in her lifetime, and that he himself had gained valuable information from her that would aid him in the similar endeavours with students he would most certainly embark on in the near (*carpe diem*, after all) future.

She was stunned for about six months, and then began compiling a list of her own. She could not, however, bring herself to take these new boys quite all the way inside her, turn them into men in the baffling factory of her body, as she never felt she'd completely expelled him from her, regained her space and balance. Fortunately, cunnilingus was trendy on campus that year, and Patrick from her Homer and the Oral Tradition class set things off, left her nipples and thighs sprinkled with scabs; he also left her an itch in the genitals and, abruptly, for a dancer, gliding and punctual, who picked up where she left off. Then there was the Jackson Heights boy who entered her life during a particularly homesick period and clung to her with one hand while masturbating with the other; he eventually confessed she looked just like a cousin he'd had an affair with years ago, thus shedding light on his anxiety regarding family gatherings. Appearing on his heels: a student from Mexico City with political aspirations who – *para mis padres*, he assured her – plucked several photos of her from her albums, and later admitted they'd flown FedEx (priority overnight) to his excessively competitive ex-girlfriend on the *calle dos bocas*; they were reunited, Luis was pleased to announce, shortly thereafter.

Interspersed between these events and after was the string of friends who overlapped, most of whom made her happy and managed to remain friends with her, and even with each other. The more possessive ones justified their overlap via her polytheistic upbringing, which must surely have turned her into an addict for options; the less possessive ones duplicated keys, and left doors and windows ajar for her to climb through at her convenience.

Kayla enjoyed the homogenizing effect of seeing head after head of boy's hair gripped between her legs. She managed to hold her interest in them because there was always that moment of pure distance, when the inextricable weave of personal history – lovers, accidents, secret pleasures, unadmitted thefts – would lift for a moment behind the boy in question, silver filaments against an empty sky. She would see herself being stitched into the pattern, a slender thread, a particular slant that he would wrap about his shoulders for an instant to warm himself with. These were the frustrating moments that drew her in, made her long to be different and for him to be the same, to be cast into a pocket of time shaped like the numerous pockets where she'd cast the others.

~

Now Tristan is there, her thighs flanking either side of his disappearing face. She can smell herself and is repelled and fascinated. Her scent clings to the air like a dark wet curtain of uncooked things: honey, mud, mushrooms. He raises his head and climbs toward her face, presses his fingers across her lips. She feels herself sinking under the weight; he edges in, punctures her paralytic glow with the flat stretch and stab of hard flesh. A particularly sharp jab in her right inner thigh makes her try to lift up and push him, but he is so heavy, and breathing isn't easy anymore, and just as she begins to cry out *Wait!* he slams his mouth over hers and her thick viscous taste rides his tongue, spreads down her own.

– Come on, he hisses. – Like a tiger.

He twists her over and the weight settles on her back. She feels her *ass* being pried apart, but her mouth is crammed with fabric and her chest run through with a series of tiny pricks and then something shimmers down between her breasts.

– I heard about Paris, he says.

She is aware of every organ of her body, its weight, pulse, and fallibility. Rectum. Kidney. The gasp of a lung. Each pain crushes into the others, becomes indistinguishable from painlessness. The pressure builds inside her, pushing against the walls of her rupturing body from the inside out, combating the pressure from the outside in.

A tree taking root, she thinks. That's all. A tree is trying to grow inside me. My mouth is stuffed with leaves, my tongue caught in the branches.

~

– It's a jungle out there, the teaching assistant had told her in a meeting regarding her last paper. – In books and out of them. And if you're going to learn anything in life, you've got to be savage about it. No habits, no hang-ups, no doors barred.

– I just don't see why that word is necessary, she'd said, her hair shadowing her flushed cheek.

– The *cunt*, he said. His tongue glistened, hit the roof of his mouth. His lips were etched across with thin lines. She was embarrassed and spun her bangles.

– The *cunt*, he repeated. – Is an integral part of *Tropic of Cancer*. You simply can't write a paper on Miller's concept of female sexuality and avoid it.

– I wasn't avoiding it, she said. – I just wasn't calling it by that name.

– No is not yes, he said. – Maybe is not yes. A cunt is not a female reproductive organ, nor is it a vagina, nor is it "her nether parts." It is a *cunt*. That is the point.

– I'm not trying to be difficult, she said, fiddling with her necklace then. –I just don't think I'd feel so good saying it.

– What we're dealing with then is, essentially, a language problem, he said. – Taboo is merely a matter of habit, Kayla. Words are sound and context. Isolated, they are not finished products. Cunt, fuck, shit. Say the words. Just say them, over and over. You'll get used to it. It might even feel good.

He reached over, laid his hand over hers, on her clavicles, stilled her fingers.

– Don't be afraid, he said. – We can open up a whole new world. His hand felt as if it had been in the sun.

– *Cunt*, she said. – *Cunt. Fuck. Shit.*

~

It is like grinding into dream within dream, each one ashing down and vanishing as it is passed – no voice, no handhold, the lead drop of lids resisting the desperate silent wail of the dreamer to *wake up! move! wake up!* She tries to cry out but her words are muffled into moans. Finally, she is able to wrench free an arm and flings it out. It hits something hard and there is a crash that is composed of thousands of tiny crashes, mirrors slamming into each other. Between them, she feels the short dense punches where her thighs meet, and then the dry glide.

– You're so tight, she hears, in huffs. – It's so good to be inside you. Shuddering and deep, still fear.

~

Her mother is afraid only of snakes. A psychic who lives in a large cedar house in the Berkshires, and owns a proportionately large dog reputed to have visions as well, told her it was because in a previous life she'd been bitten and killed by a cobra.

Kayla had seen a cobra once, swaying up from the basket of the flutist in the marketplace. She'd been four and in Bombay, and the snake's hood wider than both her hands thumbed together.

– Don't be afraid, *beta*, her uncle Deepak had told her. – The man is a charmer. The snake is under a spell and cannot hurt you.

Later that day they'd learned the snake had shot in a molten flash right out of the basket, through a swarm of mirrored saris and billowing pants, and straight for the small boy napping at the betel nut seller's side.

When her mother was still smaller, a cobra had worked its way down from the jungle to Powai Lake and killed three children. The family had remained in the house for days. As the rain beat against the roof, they'd clutched cups of spiced tea with buffalo milk and waited.

It took a long time for them to begin to feel safe again, and they never completely did.

~

Her mind is sinking into ambers and reds. She is so submerged in that glow, as if she has permeated ice or fire, that it takes a moment to realize he has passed out upon her. Slowly, her body reassembles. His breathing is deep and his exhalations push like fists into the small of her back. He is surely asleep, but she is afraid to move, afraid she has misunderstood and that he will rise and leap at her, growl his way back into her flesh. She lies perfectly still for a long time. Finally, his own breathing rolls him off her to the side.

Light seeps in through the blinded windows, casting orange stripes that drop down the wall and across his turned head, slide the length of his body and bed. The air is thick with smoke and his breathing. Quietly, she peels out of the bed and stands, her inner thighs pearling over, dank to the knees. Her jeans and cardigan lay crumpled by the crate. She pulls on the jeans, trying not to inhale the smell of the room, feels how her stomach clenches and lifts when she does. As she reaches the top button of the sweater, she grabs instinctively for her neck. Then clavicles, chest, pinching wool, and flesh, until her ribs. She begins to shake.

Her eyes torch wildly about the room. Finally, she sees it: the tiger claw's chain burning through a tawny heap of ginkgo leaves and the brilliant, shattered glass her foot has just missed.

She crouches, delicately coaxes the necklace from the jagged remains of the tequila bottle. It glitters its small weight into her palm, the chain links bouncing gilded light into her eyes. The light cuts. Her eyes sting, and with the tip of her finger she strokes the nail, acquired by a boy she never knew, and safeguarded for her for years by a woman and man who had not known her but who'd somehow treasured her in advance. She is homesick for these strangers, wants to lay her head down in a secret corner and sleep for months, dream them back into her life. How worn her uncle's body must have been that arboreal dawn. His eyes like wounds, painfully open.

She is not sure how to define what has just happened, at what point fate plays a role and nothing more can be done, at what point it was still in her hands. She tries to clip the chain around her neck, but it has lost a link and will not hook so she wedges it into her jeans pocket. Squatting, she collects the pieces of glass, being painstakingly careful as her great-grandmother taught her when, as a child in India, everything she touched seemed to long to be elsewhere: china, clocks, mirrors flashing sun to the cement floor, an earthenware vase of peacock feathers, their tumbled centres of blue, unblinking eyes. She gathers every sliver, grazes the surface for any fleck of light that could indicate a leftover splinter.

Tristan continues to sleep as she makes her way back to the bed and squats again. Tipping her palms, she pours the larger pieces of broken rubies into his bedside slippers. He does not stir as she rises into the slatted light and works her way to the door, scattering behind her a dense wake of the invisible splinters. No movement still as she twists the knob, brushes the hair from her eye, and exits.

Desilicious

In Search Of

SUNIL NARAYAN

"I love you."

I always say that right before I drift asleep on my man's well-defined pectorals. It's the tie that binds all of my Harlequin dreams together. His name and attributes are constantly in flux. Most recently his name was Jackson, the Southern heir-apparent of a sizeable fortune who owned and managed a coffee shop in a picturesque suburb outside of Boston. He lived in a gorgeous loft above the shop, around the corner from the school where I taught high school lit. That first morning I stumbled in, attempting to read the paper and dig through my pockets to pay for a bagel and coffee, and I was startled when I looked up and saw salvation staring back at me. I think we had some sort of mini-convo but all I remember was my mouth fixing itself in a permanent smile. I returned religiously the next morning to receive my communion. The coffee wasn't that great, but the lithe olive-skinned beauty that poured it sweetened the deal. By the end of three weeks, Jackson started calling me "Professor," and I began to delusionally think he might actually be flirting with me.

I bumped into him during a restless Saturday morning run down by the river. I was surprised when he stopped to talk and even more so when he asked if I wanted any company. I did my best to keep up but nearly collapsed toward the end. While walking back he stopped to brush an eyelash off my cheek, his fingers lingering a little longer than necessary, drawing my eyes to a point inside his skull. Some force of self-preservation started my feet moving again, and we ended up in front of his shop. He pulled out his keys and I followed him inside behind the counter without waiting for an invite. He turned around to open the cooler and handed me a bottle of water and a Fresh Samantha behind his back. I twisted the cap off and held it out for him as he turned to face me. His right hand brushed against mine as he reached for the bottle, but this

~ 33

time it didn't linger, but encircled my hand. I felt like I was under a heat lamp and noticed that Jackson had bridged what little distance there was between us and his left hand was now planted firmly on the counter behind me. I felt a li'l woozy and leaned back, inadvertently sitting on the counter in the process. He didn't miss a beat; by the time I looked up he was standing right in front of me, my legs to either side of him. He just stared at me for what seemed like an eternity, and my breathing felt ridiculously out of place. My right hand had unconsciously started traversing his left forearm and was now working its way up his bicep. He finally leaned in and kissed me. I didn't see stars. But I did feel like the carousel had started spinning out of control. My legs hooked in behind his knees and my right hand gripped his arm to steady myself. Before I had time to recover, his mouth had descended to the point where my neck met my collar bone and his hands were on my hips. My left hand had slipped under his Vandy T and was working its way up his torso when he immediately stopped and pulled the shirt over his head. The effect was instantaneous. I felt like a kid who had just been given the best toy in the entire store. He had a light dusting of hair on his chest and abs and a tattoo of Winnie the Pooh on his right shoulder. A nibble on my earlobe cut my appraisal short.

"If I had a teacher like you in high school I never woulda left."

He had the remnants of someone trying to hide their Southern roots. His voice exuded confidence and sexiness. It wasn't a profound statement or all that lyrical, but the delivery was impeccable and it had the desired consequence. My back arched and I drew him in even closer. A boy could get used to this.

No sooner had that last thought entered my mind when the alarm bells went a ringing. Ridiculously attractive, financially secure, seemingly intelligent, self-assured, inherent bedroom skills: something wicked this way walks. I had yet to even say anything cynical. All I seemed capable of was a goofy grin and the sudden comprehension of Chewbaka's language. Men that render my brain obsolete scare the shit out of me. Who knows what neuroses lurked behind that smile? Psycho axe killer alcoholic cocaine-whore amphetamine junkie married with newborn doesn't pay child support open relationship socks with sandals voted for Bush tighty whities flannel shirt hates spicy food thinks I speak Indian doesn't cuddle eats SPAM religiously fundamental heartbreak heartbreak heartbreak. . . .

"Musgonow. . . ."

"What?"

My trusty latent Tourette's syndrome had come to my rescue once again. I jumped off the counter and onto the other side before I could change my mind.

"Imustgo . . . gottago. Bye."

His face was completely consternated and he was speechless. His look convinced me I had made the right decision: the boy had never been rejected before. E-v-i-l. Plain and simple.

~

Sadly, that's only a minute part of the saga. It's unnerving how vivid these dreams are. And more disturbing how corny they are. It's the worst of Lifetime (Television for Women) and USA's *Up All Night* rolled into one. (Well, if I were a female for the former, and if Gilbert Gottfried were gay for the latter.) I remember conversations word for word, subtle glances, mental meanderings, sweaty palms, the anxiety and the longing. I doubt this is normal but I'm too embarrassed to ask other people if they also have a pantheon of fictitious lovers. And I don't need Freud to clarify them. I don't want to fuck my mother, I'm just lonely.

I fail to sympathize with those who trash arranged marriages. Honestly, how horrendous could it possibly be to have your parents ensure your love life? And even if it results in a loveless, sexless cohabitation, you're at least in a lower tax bracket, and your sexability to the non-spousal population increases exponentially. It's all about options and I'm slightly peeved that an ABQD in search of someone who will fuck his mind and body is somehow more ridiculous than a forty-three-year-old Silicon Valley engineer in search of an eighteen-year-old future baby factory who makes seven-course meals while playing the sitar with her *kundi* when she's not doing *Durga puja* and shining his Batas. I would totally trust my parents to find me a quality cutie, but until Hritik and Salman are captured in print by *Stardust* in the Castro, I kinda doubt *India Abroad* will give two shits about my achy breaky heart.

With no bio-data on the horizon, I'm supposed to be comforted by my friends and family, accomplishments and acquisitions. Modern philosophers such as Destiny's Child tell me to savour being an independent (wo)man and a survivor. The Tao of TLC has made me wary of scrubs and cautioned me against chasing waterfalls. Sister Mary has had me searching for real love since '93 and the gospel according to Aretha has made me demand some R-E-S-P-E-C-T. I have been primped and pruned to get up on my soapbox and sing it loud and sing it proud that I don't need no man to define me. But despite all their crooning, my gurus would be disappointed. Cuz all I really want for Christmas and the other 364 days of the year is a wee bit of romance, someone to hold me, look me in the eyes, and say, "I love you," and mean it. I want to be part of the übercouple that people hate. I want to have a first date with sweaty palms, intertwine fingers at the movies, giggle nervously at innuendo, share a banana split, have a Blockbuster night, make a mess in the kitchen, watch Saturday morning cartoons, finish his sentence, fall asleep in his arms, and wear his oversized sweatshirt in the morning.

I want a date that starts on Friday and ends on Sunday. I want to go to work late and red-eyed because he kept me up all night. I want to dress up as *Pinky & The Brain* for Halloween, show him off to Mommy on Thanksgiving, actually know what mistletoe looks like, send out overly saccharine joint holiday cards, kiss him on New Year's Eve, not mourn on Valentine's Day, hold hands during Pride, grill veggie burgers on the fourth, and try to make *palak paneer* on the fifteenth.

I have all of these elaborate scripts running around in my head, dying to be used. They're a product of my fascination with '80s romantic comedies and Brit synth pop, with a splash of Bollywood and HOT 97. I can't be the only one who sees the happy and the joy of a John Cusack/Madhuri movie set to Boy George and Bounty Killer, can I? And even if I am, tell me lies, tell me sweet little lies. The string of one-night stands couldn't even do that right. After you say, "Hello," you're supposed to move on to a dazzling display of wit or use a tired pickup line that only your charisma could pull off. "Excuse me, I seemed to have misplaced my boyfriend," or, "Interested in being my Lamaze partner?" top this list. You're *not* supposed to say, "Top or bottom?" "Your place or mine?" or ask if I'm into s&m or water sports. That's at least third or fourth date material, a few hundred pages in. I hoped that maybe one of them had just missed a cue and was doing a little improv until he fell back into character. No such luck, and I kept on searching, or fucking, depending on how you look at it. I suppose there's nothing romantic about being promiscuous, but that doesn't mean a slut can't be a romantic too. Maybe that's why I've seen *Pretty Woman* so many damn times. I'm still waiting for my turn to feel like Cinde-fucking-rella.

Repressing my feelings is tiresome. I want someone who can see through the charade I've been living out for the last twenty-three years, who understands that I'm not as aloof and unemotional as people think, someone who can forget my historical imperfections and forgive my guilty conscience yet still realizes that the four-year-old who's scared of the dark, the six-year-old who doesn't get why other kids call him darkie, the chubby twelve-year-old who's always the last one picked, and the twenty-one-year-old who cried himself to sleep for weeks after his first broken heart, are still lurking inside.

And someone who will chuck a box of Kleenex at my head and tell me to stop pitying myself after a little babying.

I want to be the last person someone dates, but not because I've died or they've died or we've died; I'm thinking less *redrum redrum* and more cute fluffy bunny. On the other hand, a few verbal smack-downs are all good and serve as adequate plot devices for passionate makeup sex. I even have the arguments all picked out (all praise to the most high *Days of Our Lives* and *Passions*): "Why did you lie to me about being a DiMera?!" or "A Lopez-Fitzgerald could never marry a Crane!" I just need someone who's down for the count. I've even got The Cure cued up for our mini-break-ups and the lotuses picked out for the reception. (I'll be damned if I let a li'l thing like sexuality get between me and my fabulous indo wedding.) The lack of a bride might throw a wrench in the Vedic proceedings, but I think two *sangeets* more than makes up for this. I couldn't care less if I lead or follow, just let me take my seven steps around the fire and change outfits a few times. Plus the idea of my man looking like a maharaja is hella hot. I won't even get into the names of our kids, but I swear they're festive.

And the survey says it's also time for me to give poor Teddy a break. Ya might think a twenty-three-year-old boy who sleeps with a stuffed animal is cutesy, but it's decidedly less cutesy when you are *that* twenty-three-year-old. Don't get me wrong, Teddy, our late-night heart-to-hearts have been a blessing, but I think it's time for me to entertain the possibility of a two-way conversation and for you to feel like a proud soccermom. We can still wax nostalgic every once in awhile and curl up to *The Golden Girls* or *Murder, She Wrote*; maybe even belt out a few off-key Disney songs. It's just that I'm a big boy now. I can go to doctors who don't entice me with lollipops and read books with no pictures. You'll always be the other man in my life and someday you can pass your ageless wisdom onto the next generation of Narayans. Teddy, I'll always be your Toys "R" Us kid, but now I want the guy in aisle twenty-three, not the BMX in aisle five.

So step up to the plate, Mister Man, and take your best swing. I'll keep pitching till you hit it out of the park and I'll look the other way if you steal my heart. Let's regress to roses are red and violets are blue and li'l brown fags can be moonstruck too. We can dance to the beat of our hearts and watch the cosmos shake in rapture at the rebirth of romance, our rhythm heralding the arrival of a love that only divine creation can outshine. I'm gonna keep on dreaming my li'l dreams and holding out hope that my knight in armour of any condition will ride in on his stallion or elephant or '84 hatchback and sweep me off of my feet. And it doesn't have to be today or tomorrow, next week or next year. I didn't get it right the first time around, but I've kicked the material boy to the curb and I'm feeling all shiny and new. I'm willing to wait cuz you can't hurry love, and until then, I'll do my thing and you can do yours, but I'll keep the light on and put an extra toothbrush by the sink just in case you turn up. And when the sunshine hits my face and I wipe the sleepy seeds out of my eyes, and I see you looking at me looking at you, maybe I'll realize that some dreams do come true.

The Lube Job

AMBER NASRULLA

Petroleum jelly. Moisturizer extraordinaire. Award-winning man repellent.

The fact is that PJ, Vaseline – call it what you will – has kept the men away from me for a while now. I've smeared it on my face to put off the hideous men with middle-parted hair who sat in my parents' living room seeking my hand in marriage.

None of them knew me. None of them even wanted to speak to me. They took one look, well, a couple – at my childbearing hips (I'm sure), my big brown eyes, and my long hair – and concluded I was marriage and chapatti-flipping material. Thankfully, the Vaseline-on-skin trick was a sure-fire way to get rid of the boys. They thought I was dirty or had gone overboard with rubbing almond oil into my hair. They thought I was exceptionally village girlish, *yaar*.

At that point, I didn't even give them a hint that I like a bit of pain, say, to be nipped on the neck. That I like to be smacked on my ass a few times in a row. If just one of those fellows, he-who-desperately-seeks-bride, had pinched or scratched my wrist, my arm, any part of my anatomy, I would have given him a chance. Believe me, I've kept the signs hidden under my *dupattas* for many years. In many locales, desi teeth have tasted my skin to the point of almost drawing blood.

~

Take Lahore – in that Punjabi city of millions I had it off with my friend Amtul's cousin, Kareem, who was visiting from California and certifiable. His bite was just right. And I've done it in London along the Serpentine in one of those stupid red-and-white-striped folding chairs that cost four quid for thirty minutes.

My friends make fun of me. "Nyla," they say, "What's with the addiction to love bites, hickeys, and bruises?" I can't explain it; I like to see *neel meri gurden pai*, into which I can push my fingers to feel the pleasure of the throb days later. I also like to listen to Indian film songs at full volume in the morning while I'm getting ready for work. The more shrill the woman's voice, the sharper her *awaaz*, the better; that's because it's not the richness of Lata's vocal chords I'm after. It's all about enduring pain.

Mmmm. Let's talk about pain. Fifteen years ago, a wasp bit me. It was my twelfth birthday when my Ami had a barbeque for me and us kids were playing *"K'ho!"* and running circles around the garden. The aunties and uncles were yakking about South Asian politics and the price of *daal* or something. I went up to the deck to get some lemonade when something scratched my neck. That spot went hot, tingled, and burned, and I was unconscious pretty quickly after that. Dropped the tray of lemonade, smashed glasses, all very dramatic. Very filmy. (Can't you just imagine a doe-eyed heroine shrieking *"Naeeee"* on cue?) Well, this little Nyla had anaphylactic shock. First time.

~

One of the guests, an uncle (not my *real* uncle), carried an Epi-Pen for his son who was allergic to peanuts. And it was uncle who, without hesitation, thrust the needle into my thigh. The pen was, I swear, six inches long and two-and-a-half inches around. That's a lot to take when you're only twelve.

Barely conscious, I watched bleary-eyed as uncle slowly pulled the needle out. I know he didn't want to hurt me but when he pulled my *shalwar* down to check to see if my thigh was bleeding and then smeared some lotion, Vaseline, I think it was, over my skin . . . I admit it, I got a thrill, my first-ever surging sex tingle.

At the hospital, a nurse extracted the stinger and gave me antihistamines and oxygen. When she left the room, I scratched the bite (and continued to do so for days) so much that it got infected. If you look close enough now, you can still see the small bump on my neck. It's my secret permanent reminder. When I run my fingertips over it now, I recall the pleasure, the absolute sonic head-rush of that first bite and the heavy ache deep in my thighs when uncle plunged in the needle. No man can ever recreate that. I mean, I've never passed out from having a man put his teeth to my throat, nibble on my nipples, or push his fortune into me. It isn't the same – no black man, no Asian, no Jewish boy who has tried, has been successful. So maybe that's why I reject the men who come to my parents' house hoping to marry me. I'm not convinced they'll live up to *the* bite. I hope that one day, one of the Nabeels, Anwars, Javeds, Mustafas, or Amirs slouched in my parents' living room will eye the petroleum jelly and feel as excited as I do. And that's when I'll say yes. That's when I'll say *bite me*.

Amber Nasrulla

Destroyer of Worlds

RAYWAT DEONANDAN

In a dream, I sit in the Clarchen Ballhaus in Berlin on ladies' night, waiting for Marlene Dietrich to slither across the dance floor, deposit herself onto my welcoming lap, tip back her top-hat, and spew a luminous funnel of unfiltered cigarette smoke from her painted lips.

In another, I am written into an adolescent science-fiction novel by Robert Heinlein, destined to fall into the arms of a domineering small-town teenage girl before I am shipped off on a rocket mission to re-conquer Venus.

In others, I am loveless and barren, forsaken and forlorn.

"I had two dreams about you this week," Tanya says. My ears prick up, more alert than anytime since a past lover's husband had unpredictably entered the apartment. "In the first dream," she continues, "we were having a coffee, then you kissed me. I had to stop you because, you know, I have a boyfriend."

"And in the second?"

"In the second dream, I didn't stop you."

"And how was I?" Her eyelids flutter and she giggles in that nasty fake baritone that only women can master. And that's where it had to end. After she's had me in a dream, how can I, a real man who doesn't go away with the dawn, compare? No ego, my friend, is that secure.

I had two dreams about Diamando this past week. In the first, I'm in the airport parking lot. I look up and see her frowning down at me from a Calvin Klein billboard; she was goddess-like in her stature and radiance. In the second dream, she and I switch bodies and begin to dance. I think it was the samba. But instead of exploring our new anatomy, all we were concerned about was who got to lead.

Illogic is the mantra of the dream state, chaos its mode and tack. Yet order springs from the jumble, a story percolates and the ego imposes a relevance oft mistaken for spirituality.

In the tradition of my people, the god Vishnu sleeps at the centre of the world, dreaming the universe, causing its being. From his navel grows a lotus, and on that lotus sits the quantum-mechanical god Brahma. Brahma opens his eyes and a world comes into existence. He closes his eyes and a world vanishes from existence. If Vishnu were to shift his colossal body in sleep, disturbing Brahma in his wakefulness, perhaps the lotus-sitter would blink, and all would be naught.

I am a destroyer of worlds, a divine egoist, the ultimate mood killer. A thousand lives blink into being with the start of my unconscious cinema, and a thousand more are quietly extinguished as I slip back into wakefulness. I am a creator of worlds, ephemeral and transient, wherein thin lives shimmer and etiolate, servicing my will yet tormenting my id.

To have dreamed a world is to have willed new life from the blackness. Contemplations on the origins of life usually begin with the accidents of electrochemistry and the violent swirling of sweet primordial soup, thick as Indian *daal*, that spits forth blobs of organic goop. From this follows the accidental collisions of simple molecules into organic strings, eventually into amino and nucleic acids, and from there to the stirrings of unconscious life.

Sometimes I wonder if we are indeed organic machines that have developed the magic of consciousness, or if we are instead pure intellect that has learned to express itself in the physical world. Perhaps there exists a vast field of intelligence, pan-dimensional and incomprehensible, that pops and percolates, occasionally protruding and projecting into the thin and inconsequential plane of physical existence. Is there, then, intelligence in every atom, a shadow of a soul haunting every quark and neutrino? If so, then we are indeed the dream, existing at the pleasure of the dreamer. All matter becomes but a state of awareness.

But these are distractions and rationalizations, paths into the darkness of intellect, away from the light of mindless beauty, that realm of intended quantum restfulness.

I dreamed once of plains of perfection, on which all failed loves repaired and rejoiced. Therein lies the power of that world, its lesson to be transported to the wakeful. Its events are plastic and nonsensical, transcending logic and reason. Yet its feel is contentment, proving that satisfaction can issue from formless irrationality. To stray from the intellect is indeed bliss.

"Tomorrow is Tuesday," Sneha whispers to me seductively through the soma ether, and I howl in laughter, as if it is the funniest joke I've ever heard. There is no sense in dream-time, no reason for sadness, humour, anger, or titillation. Emotions erupt from the id without first being summoned; there are no rules. It is a quantum mechanical thing, wherein effect can comfortably precede cause, laughter precede the joke, and love precede acquaintanceship.

Thus is the comfort of Vishnu and Brahma. They are the sleeping and sleepwalking gods, icons to the weird set of quantum formulae. Our world, their dream, is stoked by the irrational, spiced with the unpredictable, and pricked by the nonsensical.

In a dream, I lay next to my beloved, ecstatic in halcyon slumber. Her breath sings in time with my own, the cadence reaching beneath the conscious to the next dream, then below that to the dream of the fundament. Ours is an orchestra of sleep, bound in rhythm to the dance of the quantum gods, and played with love and tranquillity. My beloved arises and rubs the sleep from her eyes. She thinks to herself, "I am a destroyer of worlds, a divine egoist, the ultimate mood killer."

that beauty and non-penetration

ZAR

december canadian terrain barren and unfamiliar were the undulations
  of your chest
how suddenly
i began to think of you
as where i wanted to be accepted
forgetting almost my émigré country

wanted to at times conform to the body of you
i have
while attempting to retain the irregularity of my shape around which
i wrap this *chaadar* maroon with the orange motif circling
the circularity, the continent a bodily extension of me
upon bumping across which on the street they say *pardonnez moi*
  addressing me
and you say "my dear i am coming to visit you in quebec"

you know the power of new energy
the force of another body
lending hope
of creating pOOls of our own to drown in
and opportunities
to climb and fall over and over

i see you
see me you, under your thighs
down, up and down
trying halfway two meet
and from my bed i see my balcony hanging off one july evening
pelted by lightning bolt thunderstorm

~ *45*

that rain in heat; montreal

i become accustomed to losing
articles of clothing
that complacency instilled which was handed down in an airtight
    container carefully preserved
when the voice of my mother, her mother before her and her mother
    before
ask me with all my strength to hold onto religion, all that, tradition
i put my tongue in your mouth and my words do not roll as they once
    used to

no more can we be two sides than one
BREATHE YOU i
hesitant at first excited taking in
but having been accustomed to existing in different temperatures
you temperate remain and i being transported through air perpetually
like pollen diffusible
speaking of raindrops, i tried telling you they were never meant to be
    understood
all this while aiming integration

i have begun to prefer this mildness of flavour
yes but do not seek to go backwards
for when planted in the meeting place the place of meeting megalopolis
    already constructed: toronto
and subsequently placed alongside another with ideas already
    architectured
i was on both occasions "for my own good" warned against seeking
    unfamiliar ground

this contemplation perhaps
is too long for a relationship not having undergone
enough changing seasons especially in geography where I am hardly
    able to witness your spring upon me

too short, is also the length of that look exchanged between my eye and
     the other on a next to me pillow

arguing and learning
takes time
i have learned to dress in layers, for protection
and to take them off as required
to not fear courage that is demanded
and alienation that arises
out of standing next to industrial structures as colossal as you

Zar

however in time it happened that i stopped looking to a map of the TTC
     for every direction, journey every
once
my

          e g
     l   s

               found
                    a
                         way
                              to
                         entangle
                    in yours
soon this handholding too will not be required at all
amidst the black blue yellow security guard faces and six AM female
     factory working legs
we too will grow up to be women, men of our own, in a country
     whose?

creation is realization, a certain fusion necessary omission
laborious, must be endeavours
but not forgetting words
which made sense to us both
is that which we desire.

Hair

SUNITA S. MUKHI

My hair's grown
long and thick
like Rapunzel's
only mine's wavy
very black and velvety
(I guess, more like Draupadi's)
It's grown
so that my lover
whoever that may be
may hold on tight
and climb upon
my solitude
to nuzzle with
an adoring tongue
eager and lavish
not
tentative   hesitant
or repulsed
by the thought of, look of, odour of
taste of
my yearning
succulent
bitter-salty at first
but when yielding
vulnerable and ecstatic
heady, sweet, pungent
like plump tropical fruit.

Truth in Real-Time

ROOHI CHOUDHRY

ZOHRA'S SEXY_GIRL

sexy_girl: a/s/l? BORING. Come on, you can do better than that.

Goatee^^: OK. What are you wearing?

sexy_girl: LOL! Didn't think you could get worse than a/s/l but you just did!

Goatee^^: What's wrong with that? OK, then back to good old a/s/l. Please?

sexy_girl: OK. 16. F. Undisclosed location.

Goatee^^: LOL! Undisclosed location? What are you? A secret agent? A sexy secret agent.

sexy_girl: That's right. I'm a sexy girl by day, sexy agent by night. Very convenient.

Goatee^^: Ha ha. Tell me more about the girl then.

sexy_girl: What do you want to know?

Goatee^^: I don't know. What did you do last night?

sexy_girl: That's a new one! Let's see. Was out shopping most of the day. Spent way too much. Then I got home, changed into a little red dress, and went to a disco.

Goatee^^: Wow. Some night.

sexy_girl: Oh . . . I just like having a good time.

Goatee^^: So, wanna cyber?

sexy_girl: Oh. Hang on, BRB.

Zohra turned toward the grilled window, drawn by the roasting peanut-smoke wafting in through it. Peering out through the bars, she could see the vendor's scalp gleaming in the midday sun as he stood yelling, "*Momphali Garam Momphali*" in the street below. Skillets of peanuts simmered on his wheeled cart and the aroma overwhelmed

Zohra's room on the second floor of the *haveli*, filling her mouth with drool. Peanuts happened to be her weakness – the familiar hot cone, newsprint spotted with ghee; the kindly Afghan seller with thrilling stories of his escape from Kabul to Peshawar.

She opened her bedroom door as far as she dared and listened. No sound, save the tick of the kitchen clock, the faint buzz of the television in the next room. If she were very quiet, she might just get out and back before anyone even knew she had gone. She covered her head with a black cotton chador, taking care to tuck away each stray hair behind her ears. Reaching back toward the door, she remembered – money, of course! She pulled a chest away from the wall, easing a ten-rupee bill from a plaster crack revealed behind it. Tiptoeing past the living room, jumping at each squeak of her slippers, she reached the front hallway.

"Where do you think you're going?"

She swiveled around, heart pounding all the way to her head. "Oh, nowhere, *Bhaiyya*." She giggled, trying to defuse the situation.

"Then why are you wearing your *chador?*"

"I was just, just. . . ." Zohra floundered, her *chador* slipping as she twisted its ends into knots. "Just peanuts, I was just getting some peanuts, that's all."

"What? Are you crazy?"

"They just smelled so good."

"Stupid whore! Sixteen years old but you'll never learn." He hulked over her bony frame; just a one-handed push from him and she stumbled into a wall. His eyes grew darker as he spat: "Running around with your face naked. Just like *her.* I told Baba he should have married you off years ago."

At the sound of her father's name, Zohra jerked her head up. "You're not going to tell him, are you?"

"Maybe I should," he sneered. "A good hiding is just what you need."

Zohra watched his shadow fade as he walked back to the living room. In her bedroom, she slammed and latched the windows as loudly as she dared and turned on the ceiling fan at its highest speed to expel the seductive peanut-smoke.

Her hands shook as she lingered at the switch plate. Finally, she steadied herself enough to crawl into bed under her quilt, a broad stretch of intricate *zari* embroidery running around its edges. As the

Desilicious

border scratched Zohra's cheek now, she imagined her mother a young bride with henna fading from her feet, biting her lip as she took scissors to her wedding *gharara*. Steeled her fingers firm as she held its fabric to the quilt's edge under a needle. Eyes bright when she tucked it under Zohra's eight-year-old chin for that last time before disappearing into a starless Peshawar night.

Huddling under it now, Zohra stared for a minute at the pipes twirling in green then fuchsia on the blackness of her computer monitor. The computer. Bought because of the training course friends had convinced Baba she should take, because it would improve her husband-prospects. A girl who surely had some of her mother's adulterous genes needed extra help, they had all said. The computer's removal was her ultimate fear, threatened many times.

But for now, she was still plugged in and online. She nudged the mouse and the screensaver was gone, the window underneath it still alive.

sexy_girl: Let's go.

~

RUKHSANA'S BLACK^WIDOW

Black^Widow: I'll be leaving soon. You better hurry up if you want to please your mistress.
corpse_of_jordan: But you just got here. And I've barely begun serving you.
Black^Widow: I've been busy all day – cooking sumptuous meals for my subjects.
corpse_of_jordan: For him?
Black^Widow cracks her whip over and around corpse_of_jordan's back
Black^Widow: I've told you before. I ask the questions. You're boring me. On your knees, slave.
corpse_of_jordan: Forgive my mistake, Black One. I am still your servant as always.
corpse_of_jordan flicks his tongue over his mistress' feet
Black^Widow: And as that you will get the punishment you deserve.

corpse_of_jordan: I am yours for the taking, and the doing, Black One. Every inch of me belongs to you.
Black^Widow: I know my property, slave. You will never escape my leash.

Rukhsana ran a finger across her brow, gathering beads of sweat and brushing them off, fanning herself with her damp *dupatta*. The air-conditioning had broken down that morning, right in the middle of a relentless Dallas drought. Now, she could hear the workmen outside, bickering over the giant machines that regulated the air in the apartment complex. She marvelled at the speed with which these repairmen had been summoned and at the collection of instruments they used to attack the ailing air conditioners. In Pakistan, she remembered, it would have taken days before anyone paid attention to the stifling problem. And then, a few dusty urchins in mismatched *shalwar khameez* would have arrived, poking at machines with their wrenches and pliers, shrugging and asking for more money to return the next day and then the next. They would shake their heads at her frustration: this was a grave matter of complexity beyond female comprehension.

Her mind skipped from that to the image of another man's shake of the head. Faisal, last night, when she confessed she had run over her monthly budget. He had shaken his head at Rukhsana's explanations. Screaming himself hoarse, he had lamented his own mother's choice of Rukhsana – a wife who could not add two and two, would not understand how hard he worked for precious dollars, did not care about his hypertension or resultant receding hairline.

She had listened, as always, nodding rather than shaking her head, careful this morning to just-right his eggs and fold-smooth his paper. Today she had cooked *aloo gosht* for dinner: an old favourite, but not expensive enough to inflame him further. She had stood that morning over the boiling curry in its pot, ladle in her iron grip, churning the hard meat and harder potatoes over and under each other, slamming all her energy into scraping the garlic from the bottom as if it were Faisal's bloody scalp with hair and nail and bone mangled together as she struck again and again.

The "ping" of the computer and the oven were almost simultaneous. For an uncertain moment, she was not sure which to answer first – the chat room with its chirrup calling her to play, or the stern reminder of the oven timer. But she quickly drew her thoughts together and, smoothing her curls with one hand, used the other to delete all temporary Internet folders, washing away traces with no time for goodbyes.

In the kitchen, she took the pan with its steaming naan out of the oven, poking at their bubbling middles with satisfaction. She placed them gingerly into a hotpot and, securing its lid, ran her finger for a moment over a silver label on its side. "With Love from Uncle and Aunty Motala," it announced in neat letters. After the wedding, she had scrubbed at it with no avail; the label was a fixture from people who insisted on being remembered.

She had tried many times to forget that dingy Gulberg duplex where her parents had left her too often. The Aunty who left too early and stayed away too conspicuously, the Uncle who was always home and stayed too near. Thinking of him, a sliver of plastic from the hotpot's handle broke off between her finger and thumb. After all these years, the handle resembled a nail chewed as far back as it would go.

Now, she pushed it away as she heard Faisal's car pull into the driveway. Perfectly timed, she thought as she smiled. Just as planned.

~

MEHREEN'S KITTEN^LOVE

Kitten^Love: You know I would call you but I'd rather just talk here.
Charlotte_Web: Why? Why haven't you called me? Don't you want to hear my voice again?
Kitten^Love: Of course I do, darling. It's just that I like this right now.
Charlotte_Web: Yeah yeah whatever. You're forgetting me already, that's what it is. All that we went through means nothing to you.
Kitten^Love: Please don't say that. Let's not fight, please? You know I love you. I will call you, very soon, I promise, but I can't today. Please understand . . . I'm in a difficult spot. You know that.
Charlotte_Web lets out a big sigh
Charlotte_Web: OK OK. Well if we're not going to fight, then what else is there to do? Hmm. . . . ;)

Kitten^Love: You know what I want to do, what I always want to do.
Kitten^Love licks her lips
Kitten^Love: Let me start with your lovely white feet . . .

Thud! Thud! Thud! Mehreen's heart raced wildly as she buttoned her jeans, one button undone messing up the rest; unbutton, re-button, hair is fine, shirt is fine. Minimize, minimize, minimize, one last look around, turn key, deep breath.

"Mehreen! Why are you always locking this door?"

Before she could answer, her mother had grabbed her wrist and, chattering, led her down the hallway flooded with desert sunlight. Through the windows, Mehreen could see the tops of palm trees sprouting from the island separating highway traffic. A boy in a white robe squatted at the base of a tree, drinking from a tap meant to water the grass.

Mehreen blinked, struggling to focus through the distractions and pinpricking memories. She caught just enough of her mother's blather to grasp that this had something to do with her bridal trousseau. In the living room, a bespectacled man rose to greet her. He reminded her of pictures in textbooks of an emaciated Gandhi, except that this man was dressed in a three-piece suit.

"Mehreen *bitya*, congratulations on your fortunate match. I myself am honoured to be serving the future daughter-in-law of one of the Gulf's most prominent Pakistani families."

Mehreen muttered thanks as her mother beamed beside her. "Well," her mother exclaimed, "show us your best!"

It was then that Mehreen noticed the stack of maroon and navy and green velveteen on the coffee table. Each box had a brass latch, twinkling in the light.

"Only my best I am bringing today. Only pure twenty-two-carat gold, and such fine workmanship you have never seen."

He opened the first case and, with the air of a conjuror, held its mouth open toward them, revealing a dazzle of white silk and yellow metal. The necklace within shone in the teeming light, nauseating Mehreen with its excess. The yellow seemed to escape the box, conspiring with the sun to assault her. Its brilliance continued to kick at her stomach and she fell onto a sofa, oozing sweat.

It had only been three months since she had returned to Abu

Dhabi after finishing 6th form at St Agnes, the Welsh boarding school that had been her home since she had been eight years old. Yet it felt as though her wedding plans had been underway for at least three years. And, watching her mother now, she knew it was probably true. There had been hints in the background during her past few summer visits, but she had chosen to blot them out. Chosen to enjoy her ignorance while it lasted, to make heady plans for the future with Charlotte in hidden school corners, to pretend there was still time to realize the impossible.

Clueless, her Gulf friends had said this proposal was so wonderful, it must have been written in the stars. But Mehreen knew all too well it had been printed, rather, in ledgers and balance sheets, carefully typed into annual plans and scrawled into chequebooks. She could discern the strategy of this happy coincidence all too clearly. But everyone knew you didn't turn fate down. Not even when it came with a penis.

Now, she squinted her way through case after case of gold fury as she fought to shut her mind from its longings. Today, Charlotte's willowy form just would not stay within the confines of its chat room left behind. Her tongue and hair and breasts and belly – soft and heaving with just-taken breaths – escaped like thousands of Pandora's hopes. She floated restless through the house, taunting Mehreen with her nakedness, opening closets and sniffing at potpourri bowls, wrinkling her nose at a joke, warming her sinewy fingers on a mug of tea. And within each movement and sound, one more world Mehreen would never again know.

Slowly, as her head's throbbing eased its pressure in degrees and the blackness in her eyes cleared, she became aware that her mother and the jeweller were standing, waiting for her response. The man spoke:

"Yes, Madam, this one is a unique piece. I can tell *bitya* is too excited to speak. Yes, I think this is the right one for the wedding day. She will look like a fairy-tale *rani*, won't she?"

"Just like a fairy tale," Mehreen finally said. "Because I have never seen anything like it in real life."

Roohi Choudhry

In This Corner

KULJIT MITHRA

I see you.

You're at the back of the restaurant. I'm trying to ignore you . . . but you're with him. He's got a hand on your knee. You're giving him that look; the one that makes your eyes have a pulse all their own.

I miss that look.

Has that hand travelled up your thigh? Has he run his fingers through your hair? Does he know what you can do with your tongue?

You're not even talking. You're just looking at each other, anxiously awaiting what may come next. What do you think he'd do if he found out about me?

Cuba.

You must remember it. Of course you do. We had told our parents that we were going with friends. Which was partially true, of course. You used to be my friend. We used to be more than that.

The third night was special. I was lying on the bed and you came out of the shower with that towel wrapped around you.

I pretended I was passed out. You called my name a few times. You even lightly slapped me to check if I was awake. I continued my acting. My eyes were closed but believe me, I felt everything. I still remember how your damp towel sounded as you whipped it against the wall. The bed squeaked as you got on top of me. I peeked a little. You pressed your body against mine, teasing me, and your smirk told me I wasn't doing a good job of hiding my excitement.

And then you grabbed hold of me.

Why'd you have to come to this restaurant?

Anju is probably wondering why I am so quiet. You'd like her, Jaspreet. She's like you in so many ways. I'm thinking of telling my parents about her. I see a future with her that I couldn't have with you. It's hard, but I think I'll be able to make this work. Look at the way she cuts her food. Look at the way she takes small sips of her wine.

So much like you.

I only hope she doesn't ask me why I keep looking at the two men at the back of the restaurant. Would I be able to lie to her too?

The Train

SARA AHMED

I hear a train passing. Always introducing irony into my life, that god. You never know what he'll do next. As for me, I hate sitting on the floor of my mom's living room for this bullshit-*rishta*-dinner. If I strategically position my leg in a certain way, my tiny tattoo creeps out of my *shalwar* and gives Mr Bachelor a hefty middle fuck-you-not finger. But the train whistle helps me zone out and in my head I'm lying in bed with my last-bed-occupier. We can hear both the trains passing. The silence between us comes from knowing someone too well to even bother with small talk. The tiny window was above his bed; I always listened for the trains even when I wasn't sleeping over. The railroad tracks were always a mystery to me because I never saw any near his house. But that was just another one of those little puzzles about him that I never bothered to indulge in.

My mom's sharp eyes draw me back to my present nightmare. The man of the hour is sitting across from me and has such a decent haircut that it makes me want to heave. I feel sorry for him. Jesus, when was the last time I had butterflies in my stomach? Oh, that's easy; another one of my ex-space-next-to-my-bed-occupier. Or was it me doing the occupying? Yeah, I think it was. Regardless; so it's dark and he's sitting on the floor, Indian-style. His shirt is in the corner somewhere, crumpled up next to mine. I'm sitting on his lap with my legs around his waist, leaning back, palms down on the carpet, attempting to attain nonchalance as I face him . . . unbalanced because the goddamn carpet is giving me rug burns. Then the butterflies ascended . . . my inclination to finally look intimacy in the face.

I zone in again as my mom gives me her famous imploring stare to "please-make-some-conversation-*jaan*-he's potential." "Potential what?" I bitch back with my eyes. Hell if I'd ever fathom four different ways of going down on him. Okay fine, my mom breaks contact before I say all that, but she's a shrewd woman and she knows I'm not interested. Not even enough to fake it. I'm sitting here, a disciple in my own inferno as my mom holds court. This is why all my relationships have been fucked from the beginning. I don't get into relationships anymore to find unconditional love, or even companionship.

In every relationship I've been in, I pray, sometimes silently, sometimes at the top of my lungs, that *he* doesn't turn out to be a fuck-up so I can bring him home to my mother and be spared the humiliation of having to pretend that Mr *Shareef-zada* here actually has a fleeting ass of a chance with me. I'm too eager for my damn status to be upgraded so I can breath easily and humbly state: I'm not destitute enough to succumb to an "arrangement." That bitter word hangs visibly with distaste from my tongue, even when I say it to myself. Of course I secretly want to be able to gloat and smugly explain to my mother that my way was the best, as my imaginary and diligent husband stands beside my angelic baby girls.

Mr Potential is eating a kabob and I am thoroughly offended at his chubby, clumsy, never-got-to-third-base hands. I wistfully remember one of the first times one of my bed-occupiers drew tiny, slo-mo circles around my belly-button and then kissed it a thousand and seventeen times (or so it seemed) as I held my breath, trying unsuccessfully to suck in my stomach. I exhale now and catch *chi-chi* boy staring at me. I grimace, trying to look very, very *badmaash*. Yeah baby-boy, I will eat you for breakfast and burp you out before my cigarette is even lit. Will this night ever end? And no, I won't make any goddamn chai. That is so cliché, Jesus. As the night rolls on, I catch myself recalling how naïve I used to be: wanting the loss of individuality that comes inevitably with marriage. Adamantly denying any substance to the rumour that I might be a "free spirit." No, my whole being used to scream of fragility and neediness. I had no idea what kind of potential I had back then. At what point exactly did I metamorphose into such a *badmaash*? Suddenly I am staring intently at the cobblestone ingrained in the sidewalk leading to my apartment. I strain my eyes to find a meaningful pattern, as if that will help make sense of my eccentricity.

I crawl into bed. Silence greets me and I don't even bother to strain my ears for a train nearby.

The Reluctant Voyeur

RASHMI CHOKSEY

Los Angeles in winter.

Endless *pakoras* savoured, and chutney licked off our sticky fingers all evening. Steaming cups of masala chai consumed over the latest *gup-shup*. Boisterous rounds of *antaakshari* with snickers and roars at double-entendres galore.

Another rowdy queer desi party comes to a close.

It's 2:30 AM. Some brave souls leave despite the freezing rain and slippery roads outside. The rest of us, three in all, decide to sleep over. The ever-resourceful host furnishes several warm blankets and a sleeping bag; we unzip and roll out the sleeping bag into a makeshift mattress and settle into his living room. The TV and VCR are still on, playing that old-time favourite, *Anaamika*. Flickering images from the screen dance across a row of three sleepy faces as I rapidly fade out.

Dead-tired and half-asleep, dreaming hazily of Jaya Bhaduri singing *"bahon mein chale aao"* to my Sanjeev Kumar, I am suddenly brought back to consciousness by movements near me. My two fellow guests are sucking face and making out like there is no tomorrow. Right there on the mattress I'm sharing with them! One is a pretty butch boi, always confident and poised in her charm. The other is a self-confessed virgin, who usually goes on and on about how she is saving herself for *the* one. I guess her resolve has crumbled. Or maybe she has found the *one*? After all, they both did confide their crushes on each other to me earlier that evening.

What starts out as a few kisses escalates to a fever pitch and before I know it, I'm hit by the raw hunger of their desire mere inches away: arms encircling each other to make sure they don't get farther than a breath away. Hands yearning to discover places they had longed to touch all evening. Mouths stifling moans, lest they wake me up. I can only imagine the dance of hands and tongues as I face the other way pretending to be sound asleep. I figure it will go on for a little while and they will postpone consummating their tryst for another time. Tomorrow is going to be a busy day and I so need these few hours of sleep. Little do I know that the night has just begun for these two passion-afflicted souls. What's a girl to do?

As I lay next to the writhing mound of entwined arms and legs barely covered by the blanket, my mind inexorably wanders to those moments of passion I have experienced in the past. My first kiss, lips swelling to meet waiting lips, tongues swirling and probing the sweetness of each other's mouths. That excruciating need to strip off all clothes and feel the expanse of her hot, aroused flesh against my hands and body. The intoxicating knowledge of having one's desires reciprocated just as feverishly. As the fervor of my two bedmates increases, I can almost feel the full figure of my lover in my arms, smell the sweet scent of her skin on mine. My tongue pulls itself out of her mouth and begins its determined journey south, stopping to taste her rosy nipples along the way, losing itself in its ultimate destination, her hot, soft, wet folds.

I am shaken out of my lustful dream by a rude whirring sound and something wet and cold plopping upon my lips. There it goes again. And again. Startled out of my slumber, I discover the culprit – the ceiling has succumbed to the force of the downpour on the roof and is steadily leaking onto our makeshift bed. The *Anaamika* videotape I had fallen asleep to has come to an end and is noisily rewinding. That explains the whirring sound. I scramble to unplug the TV and VCR lest they get soaked too, keeping my face turned away from my bedmates, who are now strangely silent.

The Roof at Chotoma's House

NEELANJANA BANERJEE

They stand sturdily on the platform of the train station, my *Chotoma* and *Mamu*, without smiling. I wave to them once. It is a small, curt showing of my hand through the barred train window. I want the train to pull away quickly so the rush of air can soothe the red that burns in my cheeks. I stare directly ahead to the empty seat in front of me. But from the corner of my eye I can see them standing, outside, rigid, in the bustle of the station.

Chotoma's chiffon sari stands out in its varying pastel shades of purple, matching the range of lipsticks she keeps locked up in her cabinet. This day she wears a light, silvery purple that frosts her lips an unnatural shade, so that they are noticeable from far away. She stands hunched as she always does in public because otherwise she would be at least two inches taller than *Mamu*. His thick glasses pick up the glare from the sun and perfectly round beads of sweat are forming on his bald head. Together they are just bits of reflection in the edges of my vision and I urge the train to move forward.

On the drive to the station, there was thick silence because Fernando, the driver, was weaving through a herd of goats. I sat between *Chotoma* and *Mamu* in the back seat. She held her large leather purse across her lap with one hand and gripped my left hand firmly in the other. I spent most of the ride looking down at my small hand in her large, rough one. I wondered why her hands were so rough as she never did any of the cleaning or cooking. *Chotoma* ran a tight household, had different servants for each task, and kept them fearful of her. She always spoke sharply to them, and they were not allowed to talk amongst themselves, much less to guests. I didn't realize this at first and would try and speak to them, asking their name or trying to share the heaping plates of sweets that *Chotoma* would leave for me. They would smile shyly at me but shake their heads vigorously and back out of the room as quickly and silently as they had entered. One of the younger girls, who couldn't have been more than twelve, whispered her name into my ear once when she was bringing me a glass of sweet *lassi* in the afternoon, but so inaudibly that I thought she had somehow spoken inside my mind. Rupa, she breathed, and then she was gone, making me realize how lonely I was for sweetness like that.

This morning, while I was packing my suitcase to leave, I could tell that the servants were taking turns looking in at me through the slight crack in my bedroom door. I could hear the swish of their feet as they pushed each other out of the way to look in on me. I stopped folding my new orange and black *salwar kameez*, a gift from the boutique that *Chotoma* liked to frequent, and turned towards the door. I felt like I was on stage and flung one hand across the curve of my forehead and careened around the room, letting go my best melodramatic wails of anguish. I remembered the flashing-eyed heroines whom I would watch on the one Calcutta television channel in the long afternoons as *Chotoma* snored loudly. I wondered what they thought of me, these wide brown eyes that peered through cracks. I wondered if they made up stories about romance and intrigue about what had happened. I finally smiled and shook my head towards the door, hoping that they understood my joking, and turned back to my packing. While I was folding my underwear, a collection of lace bras in black, cream, and, blue and bikini cut panties, I realized what they must think of me and wanted to cry.

The night before, I fell asleep quickly, the way I always do when I am upset. When my *Dadi* lived with us and would watch me crawl into bed for a nap whenever I was scolded, she told me that I got this trait from her. She said it was a good habit to have because sleep is always an easy escape from one's problems. Most nights I was at *Chotoma* and *Mamu's*, I tossed in bed and sweated through my long nightgown. The mosquito netting blocked the fan and only let in a hot puff of air like someone's breath. I found myself conjuring ghosts from my real life. Oceans away, my friends were doing mundane things like driving down familiar streets without me. I would stretch out in different ways along the large bed and think about a young wife on her wedding night, the darkness and the sweat and the looming danger of a husband beside you. I would imagine being a woman who had never been touched.

Now, after all that has happened, I closed my eyes tight, turned on my left side, and slept quickly, not wanting to see the tea-coloured hands that followed me into my dreams. In the middle of the night, I found myself suddenly awake, my heart beating fast as though I had heard a noise. I looked into the dark corners waiting for a shape to materialize, but there was no movement except for the distant fan. In the morning, when I rose thick-eyed and forgetful, I found the doors locked from the outside. I pulled the handles and pushed, then banged with the flat of my palms and yelled loudly and flatly in English, "Let me out! Hey! Let me out of here!" Then I heard the jangle of *Chotoma*'s keys, unlocking the padlock she had used to keep me in.

I hadn't cried when she had found us on the roof. I hadn't even noticed because my eyes were shut so tightly and there was so much in the air around us that her presence couldn't even touch me. Shareen and I were sitting in the last corner of sunlight on the roof. He had found me there, with my head tilted back and the sleeves of my yellow and blue *salwar* pushed up as far as they could go.

"What are you trying to do?" he had asked. "Get darker? Don't you know what they say? A fair-skinned bride is worth twice her weight in gold."

I feel healthier with a tan, I replied, keeping my head tilted back. Where I'm from, you're lucky if you see the sun in December.

He sat down on the gravelly ledge next to me. I didn't look at him because his knee was resting against my thigh, causing my heart to beat fast, and I knew that my eyes would catch like they had been doing for the last three days he had been home. Instead, I looked into the bamboo grove behind the house and tried to count all the different shades of green I could see. Below us, there were high shrieks of girls' laughter and the patter of feet. I listened to this game every day and recognized the *digga digga* chant that the girl who was chasing had to make.

"What game are they playing?" I asked.

"It's called Old Woman's Fingers," he explained. "One girl has to chase the others and catch them and take them back to her hut, which is a circle drawn in the dirt. But they can escape with the help of the free."

I listened again to the steady chanting. "Why does she have to make that noise?" I asked.

"That's how you know who is chasing you," he said. "Who to run from."

I looked over at Shareen then and he was staring straight at the roof of the house across from us. His hair had a curl in the back that reminded me of pictures I had seen of my father when he was in college. A mosquito buzzed loudly in my ear and I shook my head in alarm.

"Oh, I brought this for you," Shareen said. "The mosquitoes are bad at dusk and I knew you'd be up here."

He pulled a tube of Boroline cream mosquito repellent from his pocket. "This is the only stuff that works on Indian mosquitoes," he said, opening the tube and squeezing the thick cream onto his fingertips.

Then he was rubbing it onto my bare arms, pulling my left arm straight and working the cream into my skin with all ten of his fingers. I sucked in air and smelled the strong odour of the Boroline, poison covered with the smoothness of sandalwood. Shareen moved quickly to my right arm, pulling it across my body and massaging up and down so that I could feel the wind of him against my breasts. His face was stern and he held his bottom lip tightly between his teeth so that it had begun to lose colour. My skin was getting warmer from the rubbing of his hands, the proximity of his face, and the blazing sun that seemed to be setting right into the roof we sat on. He stopped for a moment to squeeze out more cream, which he smeared onto my neck.

"The mosquitoes can be really bad at this time," he whispered.

I closed my eyes because his hands were stroking my neck in a way that brought the sun closer. Later, I tried to go back to that moment, back to when his hands first started to travel the circumference of my neck, trying to find some thoughts that were rational. For a moment when *Chotoma* was screaming at me in a voice she reserved for the firing of servants I tried to imagine that I had thought, this is wrong. But really, my lips were already swollen when he pressed his own against them.

Chotoma hadn't come up the long, darkened staircase right then. Perhaps if she had, we would have heard her and pulled away from each other quickly and she would have frowned at us. Maybe then she would have kept me closer to her side for the rest of my stay and sent Shareen on more errands or thought up some complex excuse for him to return to university earlier. But she didn't come right away. She had been looking for a green blouse of hers, which she wanted to wear for dinner under her new specialty embroidered sari. And she wasn't loud and grunting on the steps as she usually was, maybe because she thought no one was around to give her sympathy. But maybe she was and we just couldn't hear her.

While *Chotoma* was in her room, with the curtains drawn and the fan on high, standing only in her underwear with her hair down, holding saris against her sagging skin, humming to herself, her son kissed me. As she rifled through drawer after drawer of large blouses cut with high backs, some with permanent dark sweat stains under the arms, he kissed me again. Then *Chotoma* covered herself with her long flowered robe and opened the doors to her room and called for her servant, Chandie, and began to yell about her blouse. But no one answered because Chandie was at the market picking up some sweets for dessert and all the others were in the back working on dinner. By then, I had reached up to thrust one hand into the curl of Shareen's hair while the other was held tight against his left bicep. By the time *Chotoma* had worked herself up enough to climb the stairs to the roof, all the while grumbling about how she was going to fire Chandie and the rest of them, Shareen's hands were kneading the flesh over my ribs and his mouth had moved to kiss the round thrust of my collarbone. So what *Chotoma* found along with her missing blouse was her niece and her son entwined in the red dusk of her rooftop, our legs jumbled and our mouths and chins shining with each other's wetness.

She dragged me down the stairs then, her fingers leaving blue lines on my wrist for a week. *Chotoma* led me to my room where she whispered about indecency and poor upbringing and shame.

"Shame," she hissed, "shame on you, dirty girl, seducing my son." As she paced the room, drawing a circle in the dust of the floor around me, her robe loosened and her breasts swung at me from the stretched and discoloured bra she wore. The lines of her face seemed as sharp as the long blade the servants used to cut coconut, but she struggled to keep her voice low. My heart beat fast and my cheeks burned and burned. She repeated the same words over and over, talking only of shame on the family, about what the neighbours would say, how she could never show her face in the market again.

"You've ruined his life," she said, her face so close to mine that I could see the way her gums were turning black at the base of her teeth. "Who will marry him now? Who will marry him when they hear about you?"

"But we were only kissing," I said, breaking the safety of my silence. *Chotoma* stopped pacing then and raised her sweaty palm up and swung it at my face, stumbling a little with the force of it; a puff of air that blew the wisps of my hair. I wish that I could have felt her slap across my face, perhaps with her bangle cutting into my lip. I clenched my teeth together because I wanted to spit in her face, shove her so she'd fall back against the old wardrobe. But she looked small and old and dishevelled and I felt a sudden wave of nausea and bit my lip hard to keep from throwing up.

"You stupid girl," she said, louder now, "you stupid girl. I know how you were raised. And now I see it, letting boys touch you. You dirty, stupid girl. I want you out of my house."

That night, the servants brought me a tray of food in my room. *Mamu* knocked on my closed door while I was eating. I went to the door and opened it. He stood there in a suit that looked too big for him and shifted on his feet. He wiped his forehead with a handkerchief that had flowers embroidered in the corners.

"You will be leaving tomorrow on the eight AM train," he said. I nodded and looked at him. He gave me a wan kind of smile and opened his mouth to say something and then closed it. "You should finish dinner and pack," he said, walking away, the soles of his dusty shoes squeaking a little.

I lean my head against the rusting bars of the train window as fields rush past. I try and breathe out the thickness of the last few days. Instead I take in the smell of coconut palms and the spice of the snacks the hawkers are selling and the acrid odour of the rust on the bars, a smell like the taste of blood.

Neelanjana Banerjee

Metal Pleasure

AZIZA AHMED

I want to write an essay about being fucked. Really good. So good I practically cried. So good I came five times. Except I can't. 'Cause it's never happened. That ultimate attainment of ecstasy. But I finally figured out why. 'Cause I'm counting on someone else to do it. Now, I could be the good feminist I am supposed to be and say, "But have I really discovered my flower? Have I searched my vagina long and hard?" Perhaps there is an element of self-blame in that. I've explored. I know. I know what my pussy looks like, fresh, half-eaten, and chewed. I know what it looks like when I wake up in the morning. I've known since I played those games with those other little girls when we were seven, eight, don't really remember now. It's just sometimes I can remember how good I used to think that felt. And there isn't a touch like another person's touch. Like another person's hand, mouth. Like another person's stroke. Sometimes even when you know that stroke isn't even good.

I mean – don't get me wrong. I've had orgasms. I've had great orgasms. But I'm talking about the multiple orgasm. And I'm talking about this dick. This guy. I hate the word guy. Like the one inside me now.

And now. Should I blame myself 'cause he fell asleep? I don't think so. But then it's over when it's over. I still have no control. Do I have the ability not to do it with this person again? Or get up and go to another? Perhaps. But that's not what I'm writing about.

I'm writing about the drive to screw this person. I'm writing about wanting to come and coming so close with one particular person – and them forgetting you didn't ever come – before their eyes drift into a sleepy world of hot air and bliss and empty thoughts and you get pissed.

I jack myself off regularly. I know what makes me feel good. I know what makes you feel good. Except you probably don't want me to try. I've come up with a couple of good reasons why this doesn't work. Why sex makes me raw and doesn't feel good anymore after five minutes.

It's psychological. It's religious. It's the desi tight cunt syndrome that prevents you from laughing during sex. That prevents you from letting yourself get as loose as you want. It's the thought of God and hell. It's the thought of the Holy book. It's the randomness of your mother popping into your mind, crying out of shame and guilt. "Is this how we've raised you?" Apparently.

The thought of being watched. It's the knowledge that the guy who belongs to the dick that's inside you might tell his desi best friend, who might tell your other friend, who might tell that girl who likes to talk, who will tell her boyfriend, who is also Muslim, who will tell his dad who's "real down" that you were with (insert boy's name here) at five-thirty when your mom thought you were at Seema's house making samosas for all your friends. Hopefully Seema is having better times than you. 'Cause, *you* know, she's not deep-frying either.

Stress. That'll block any orgasm. It's that realization that the wall you are looking at, white, holes from thumbtacks, the holy pendant tossed on the table 'cause the sharp edge of the *alif* was cutting him when your chests rub together – it's all distracting. And the wall isn't even that exciting. It's barely distracting. It shouldn't be as exciting as what's going on behind you that he is screaming about.

And you moan for fun, 'cause it's supposed to be fun. Or perhaps it's the ceiling that's distracting. It's the fact that you thought that the mirror and beaded artwork that is stuck onto the ceiling, staring down when he sleeps, was "perfect," making him original and creative. Who else would fall asleep looking at mirrors and thread and cloth from his parents' home country? Pakistan.

But do they even do this in Pakistan?

And you lay on your back. Perhaps that's too cliché: you got with him 'cause he was creative. Does there need to be a better reason? But the truth's the truth. Not creative enough apparently.

You wonder if the red-green-purple-gold cloth was stitched by some child. You can trace the *zari* work in your mind. In, out, in, out. It's supposed to feel good. Five orgasms at a time. How about one orgasm at a time? How about my own hand getting me off?

You watch the glint of metal on the floor. The shine of sliver. The thin necklace. The sharp edges of the curved script, containing the only name my parents would allow me to wear against my skin. Would the cool metal of the sacred pendant feel alive against my . . . I want to feel what I cannot say, cannot write.

The first smile. The first groan. The first laugh to escape my lips.

He looks confused. Why now?

Maybe I'll try when I get home.

January 2003

PRASENJIT MAITI

I seek the silences of your thighs, Calcutta, my expanse and my
dwindling fury, as I spit on my grave and look back over my shoulders
like my hunchbacked worries . . . I steal your lines and lose my job and
kill our children and come sooner than your desire. . . . The morning
tram droops an early, hopeless return while the winter wraps around
our windshield in and out the vanishing green . . . I walk back home in
the company of mists and memories of battles and happen to wag my
tail and my tongue when I run into my god. . . .

Sex, Lies, and Hash Pakoras

MILAN BOSE

We've drifted apart and don't really hang out that much anymore, yet lately I've been drawn to my single desi girlfriends in their thirties – we share a common bond of overwhelming guilt drifting down the phone line every time we speak to our parents and they ask, "So did you meet anyone?" My Big Fat Indian Wedding and all that.

Brunch at Jane's on Houston has been a bit of a ritual, if you can get a table. In grand *Sex and the City* style, I was meeting the three surviving charter members of the New York chapter of my International Board of Advisors for some post-yoga pancakes, low-fat yogurt, and chit-chat. The topic *du jour*, as ever, was our so-called sex lives. Rushika breezed in and started to talk immediately as if finishing a sentence held over in time and space from a previous conversation, commandeering a coffee already ordered for her in expectation of this sort of behaviour. This was the full Rush. Resistance was futile.

Rushika was a delicate, bird-like jewellery designer living in the Village with two overfed cats and a ten-year, on-again-off-again relationship with a St Mark's Place tattooist named Brian, who had some generic last name that no one could ever remember. I knew her sister at college and "socially adopted" her eight years ago when she moved to the city. She was from San Fran and took it upon herself to be the voice of bohemia in our little collective. Though she grew up in the burbs like the rest of us, she enjoyed shocking us, or at least trying to, with her tales of the street, hook-ups, exotic piercings, and other stuff kids got up to these days, delivered in nonchalant everyone's-doing-it tones. What kept her in our orbit was, unlike her other friends, we knew where she was from, her *mummi-ji*, *dadi-ji*, aunties, and *chachas*, her brown basement carpet littered with old Indian movie mags and her *puja* obsessed grandmother for ever making her eat *prashad* that came as dubious lumps of brown sugar and hard rice, for no good reason. We knew about how when she was six she thought Chachi was really Indian and the Fonz and Amitabh were really the same guy. We were a tether to that world. Rush was a fantastic source of mad stories, ridiculous and increasingly improbable sexploits drawn from her random grab-bag of friends forever dropping by for three months and living on her pull-out Ikea sofa. She also baked the best hash *pakoras* in lower Manhattan.

"This Indian guy thing is, like, *totally*, out of hand," pulling down from the ether, a topic weighing on all of us, like a cable-TV clairvoyant.

Rush had started talking like a valley girl these days, ever since her twenty-one-year-old sister and her friends from L.A. had come to stay, infecting her with their west coast syntax. We pretended not to notice, hoping it would go away on its own.

"I mean like, what is the big deal? This pressure thing is, like, bullshit. It's not like our parents are going to live our lives for us. We're different people and we can't expect to live up to some post-Bollywood fantasy they have in their heads. In the end we'll suffer for it, like we always do. Like, just look at Arundida."

We had begun to refer to Arundida as if she were dead and not just married and living in Notting Hill. She had become our cautionary tale. A friendship, a life reduced to a brunch-time anecdote.

Arundida was the fifth member of my board who got married last year. Yeah, and she married Indian: Rakesh, a harmless but crushingly boring banker who was at least thirty pounds overweight and kind of reminded me of a Punjabi George Costanza, except without the neurotic humour that made short men bearable. Rush, when she first met him on one of her parentally imposed "set-ups," said his oversized blazer and brown loafers reminded her of a dirty uncle at community functions – the sort who lurked on the edges checking out teenaged girls. When she first slept with him, it was at her place on her Mark-smelling, 200-count sheets, surrounded by scented candles; it should be said, they'd already been "dating" for three months. She was high on some new Jamaican blend her neighbour brought her, and it was only the thrill of transgression that got her through it. The sex wasn't terrific, but better than she expected. He made love like an unattractive guy, sweetly and with great care as if he were just happy to be there. He wept after he came. She confessed afterwards this made her feel maternal towards him and decided then and there she could marry him. He'd do.

How could she accept this? I was indignant on her behalf. She went both ways on it. We'd talk late into the night in low phone voices, like teenagers, coming up with new spins on the situation. We discussed the engagement to death. See, after seven years of Mark and the heartache, family crisis, and slow-motion break-up, Arundida couldn't disappoint her parents again. Her father had angina and wasn't supposed to live long and her mother was one of those maternal guilt machines, on the phone three times a week with the same message. To be fair, the pressure was relentless, and Arundida was worn out. Two years out of a serious break-up and seven months of $200/hour therapy, she finally gave in and agreed to marry him. The wedding was your typical South Jersey affair, more his family than hers, held in a Gujarati banquet hall, complete with an inaudible pundit who went on forever and the requisite buffet style veg dinner officiated over by a slick desi DJ improbably named "Goldy" or "Mike." Not enough of her friends could attend. Though we talked about it for ages, I never quite made it to India for the religious ceremonies which was just as well, as I heard they were just depressing – with his South Delhi aunties complaining within earshot that she was too dark, too old, and generally not good enough for their golden boy with his Goldman Sachs income and his Wharton MBA. As if.

They didn't know what *she* was giving up. They didn't know who she was, that she put herself through Columbia law school, secretly paid the health insurance when her father's illness became advanced, saved Cuban refugee families from deportation, finished near the top of her class, helped us all through our countless banal crises, and built a great reputation as a trade lawyer in one of the best crusty old-boy firms in the country not known for promoting women, let alone minorities. She was so much: sexy, smart, worldly, and most of all, entirely self made – she spoke French with an endearing Québécois accent, and despite an early accident and a painfully torn ACL, she became a master of the red runs as a snowboarder; she was also a talented salsa dancer, a bit of an expert on Kieslowski films and, if anyone asked, could make a mean paella. They didn't know that she could have married better men – men who would have been only too glad to have her, who would have deserved her. Men she turned down. No, they knew nothing of this. It didn't matter to them.

We were best friends for three years. Through law school, we shared clothes and living space and, it must be said, we shared men. We were sisters in the finest sense.

She knew I never approved of her choice.

We fell apart after the engagement. Now, since the wedding, I've been downgraded to the "hey girl how are ya" emails and the requisite mass-mailers of jokes and anodyne travel summaries written in that recognizable bi-level voice, that could read by feared "aunties" as acceptable behaviour for good married girls, when they were eventually leaked by mendacious cousins.

There is less to say now.

As if we both recognize she's in violation of the rules of our pact with life. She moved to London and fell off the conference call, as it were. Whatever. . . .

Rush continued:

"So, like, what does it mean?" she asked no one in particular, actually addressing the table of boho couples across from us. "What are you really, really after with an Indian guy? What is Indian, anyway? It's not a place, it's just a sensibility, an understanding, but why can't you get that from other non-Indian guys who just understand what it's like to be outside, to be other?"

Rush dipped into her repertoire of deconstructionist riffs while getting philosophical about relationships. She had her psychoanalysis phase a few years ago and now was moving into a Gaytri Spivak moment. It all depended on who was staying at the apartment, really.

These were all good questions that none of us really knew we had the answers to. We just knew that it meant disappointing some part of ourselves if we didn't at least try. The "White Wedding" fantasy dies hard in women raised here.

"Well. . ." I offered, trying to gather my thoughts before Rush could interrupt again, "I want:

• Someone who will understand my family . . . and the way I relate to them . . . I just don't want to explain . . . I'm tired of translating . . . I don't want to do that for the rest of my life. . . .

• Someone in touch with things desi who doesn't mind kicking back to an old Dilip Kumar flick from the sixties or *Kuch Kuch Hota Hai* on a raining Sunday night . . . that's all I'm asking for. . . .

• Someone who'll never hold who I am against me, whatever happens. . . ."

Rush had her response well prepared as she sat up straighter, shifted her napkin, and in her best high school debating society falsetto, said, "Okay, let's say you *want* to date Indian men. Where are you going to meet them? You've lived here ten years and you probably know most of the eligible Indian boys who were in our years at school. There aren't that many of them in their mid-thirties anyhow. There are lots my sister's age. Let's face it – we're generationally screwed."

"Get online, girl!" Mitu exhorted.

Online dating – while its time may have come, I've never really warmed up to it. We all surfed, and I have thought of putting up a false profile on Nerve, just to see who responds, but never took it seriously. This was desperate chick territory. Or was it? Besides, I've never had trouble meeting men. At least, that's what I say to myself.

"What if anyone from the community recognizes me?" I said. "It's a total avowal of personal failure – all those aunties who resented the fact I did well and got ahead will be gloating forever. I can just hear them prattling on about how Ritu Kapur's daughter can't get married: 'Arre . . . she went to a good school, and is a lawyer only, but now look at her, living in New York with these boys and still can't get married at her age. It is what happens when they are given too much scope to do that dating, shmating. It has given them false hope, and now look – who will marry her now. Poor Ritu has no influence on her. God willing, my Monica, the same age, is settled. And her second is in grade one. It is quite sad, poor Rita. . . .'"

My monologue ended weakly, and I lost myself in a break-up conversation a few tables over, one of those, "It's all about me, not about you, can't we just be friends" routines.

Rushika offered, "Yeah, the guys on these sites are big losers: a sorry collection of mama's boys, skid-marked computer nerds with green cards and sky-high Madhuri Dixit expectations. There are no cool ones on these sites. Do you blame them? Who would go on next to some loser from Bangalore looking for someone to look after his nightmare mother?"

These days, Mitu spoke almost exclusively in tele-parables: "And with the professional desi boys in their thirties, Mr Bigs are a dime a dozen, while Aidens are rare finds . . . and where are the edgy boys or the sexy, outdoorsy guys who still know how to get into sketchy jazz joints in Brooklyn?"

"They're dating white chicks," I offered in my bitchy voice.

"No, they're all twenty-six!" Rush laughed.

"Damn, nothing wrong with dating down, girl!" Mitu chimed in that rhythmic mock ghetto-cadence.

We all knew that Indian boys had to be older or a least within a few years of our age if it was to be acceptable. Plus, I'd never been out with anyone much younger; I don't think we'd have much to talk about. I'd find reasons to feel old. I'm a creature of my peculiar generation and every time I saw his friends, listened to his music, I'd feel old, and there wasn't anything he could do about it. These were guys who grew up amongst video games and *Lara Croft*, while I was more Duran Duran and *Melrose Place*. So, as pretty as they are, it's just not worth going down that path.

Mitu continued, dropping the "girlfriend" tone. "I can't date Indian boys. It's like dating my brother or something. There is something vaguely incestuous about it, don't you think? I get visions of my parents doing it when I think of it. I know it's warped, you can't rule out have a billion people like that . . . but it's true."

"What about Aamir?" I said, putting it out there and then doing a wincing mental check to recall if everyone was supposed to know this.

"He's different. He's a Muslim boy, sort of taboo. My parents would have freaked, and besides he was gorgeous, way out of my league, and a total modelizer. We only got together once, and I was really drunk, but . . . I'd do it again." Mitu laughed inappropriately, and quite unselfconsciously – drawing the attention of the boho brigade. I envied the way she could lose her self like that, in the moment.

Mitu was an investment banker "resting" on a fat severance package doled out after her desk downsized last year, and was still was undecided about where to go next. She was originally from Boston and did English lit as an undergrad, learned Spanish in her third year as an excuse to meet Argentinean men, and ended up surfing the boom covering Latin America equities. She was a writer at heart, but figured it wouldn't keep her in her Manolos. Also, she figured, she had missed that boat when she turned down an unpaid internship at the *Village Voice* in favour of Morgan Stanley's training programme and a lifestyle that allowed her to pay back her college loans without stressing her parents.

"Look, lets face it, thirty-something Indian men are basket cases. I don't know what you expect. If they're not married by that age there's a reason. They're damaged goods. It's a cliché now. Indian men tend to be privileged, chronic commitment-phobes who wouldn't know great women if they were run over by them. They don't know what they want. They are our communities' Woody Allens – self-obsessed, passive-aggressive, and repressed beyond belief. I don't want to be Mia Farrow." Fair point.

"Most Indian boys in their thirties are serially dating white women, who can handle their shit, before they end up settling with some young desi from Jersey who doesn't know any better."

"Well, it's better than the banker boy who marries the white chick after head-fucking with desi chicks he'd never marry because of his fucked up baggage," Sara offered, in a uncharacteristic burst of profanity, once again attracting the attention of the chino-clad table next to us. I'm sure they'd never heard brown girls talk like this before.

I was never sure how to take Sara. We shared a lot but on this topic – dating desi – but she was a bit hollow to me. I somehow felt I never quite got close enough to her. She was the sort of gorgeous and ridiculously confident super-woman you couldn't help but admire, yet at the same time worried her Nigella Lawson-meets-Hillary Clinton façade masked deeper issues.

Sara was an assimilator. Her way of coping with her otherness was, for many years, just to blend in. Extremely fair-skinned, she passed for white much of the time. A friend of mine from college who had gone to high school with her was surprised to learn she was Indian at all. She apparently passed herself off as Jewish. We all knew this, she'd admitted as much, and we recognize the impulse – in our honest moments, some of us might have done it if we could have gotten away from our brownness like that. But it separated her from us. And she knew it.

Sara has been dating a steady stream of emotionally unavailable Viking men, all of whom seemed to share the disconcerting trait of staring off into the middle distance whenever she tried to engage them in conversation. She's quite clear, she wants designer kids; it's her way of assimilating – an act of physical integration she always sought. She didn't want brown babies with complicated names who'd stand out, even a little, like she did. She wanted to procreate into the social register – hyphenated kids with exotic yet mainstream looks, with sexy polo circuit names, with all the toys she never had, with all the acceptance never fully granted to her in her lily-white school. She wanted a super-kid, a product of two double Ivies and the power of two traditions – everything doubled in a hue of light golden brown. She was in love with the thought of being in love with her baby.

Anyway, we all knew the lines, or something close: desi boys were mama's boys, lily-livered, chicken-shit, dough boys who you can't trust or look up to – or something like that. This was a female character in Srinivas Krishna's *Masala* talking. It was the first time I heard Indian men described in this way and it resonated with me and my college-aged girlfriends. As did Salman Rushdie's point about Pakistani women being much more impressive than Pakistani men. So what *is* it about Indian men? Not quite the masculine ideal – skinny legs, distended pot-bellies, questionable body hair sprouting from every orifice, notoriously unfit, middle-aged spread waiting to explode just months after adolescence. Not a pretty sight. Not everyone's bag.

And yet.

Somebody had sent me an article from a London paper I meant to circulate to the collective. It was about the new celebrity penchant for sub-continental men from Diana to Liz Hurley – something about them being reliable and grounded in family values, but still urbane. Just the type, if you're a distressed celeb, you want as surrogate dad to your kids after your latest James Dean-esque wastrel left you for a twenty-four-year-old.

But where did such news leave us? I'm not quite sure I buy into the pessimism. I'd been to Goa, to Dubai and Chandigar, and seen sexy Indian men, the tasty, immaculately groomed Jet Airways steward, the sleek bartender in Bombay with his razor-cut hair and yummy abs. Or more substantially, this delicious guy, Ravi, whom I met at a wedding a few years ago in Jaipur, with these dimpled eyes, a mesmeric voice, speaking in these hushed tones, with a kind of faultless, authoritative accent, about an early childhood education project he'd helped set up – he was humble, sexy and, respectful, but of course – married! If I'm honest, he remains my mental standard, after, of course, Shashi Kapoor in the 1960s. Every once in a while I get a glimpse of a Ravi – at an art opening, at yoga or a dinner party – just often enough to keep my hopes alive. For whatever reason, I can't give up on this ideal. Rush thinks it's crazy and that I need to "up my dose." It's my narcissism gone awry. I'm looking for a male version of myself – and if I weren't so self-loathing, I'd see how damaging all this idealism was for someone with an ever-diminishing supply of fertile, Indian-sex-goddess-eggs! I'm not so sure.

Then it happened. Back at our table, Rushika stopped in mid-sentence again as two impossibly, and almost depressingly, sexy desi boys, with their gym bags and carrying armfuls of newspapers, sat down at the now chino-free table beside us. And, like that, our conversation sputtered off of its confident riffs and right there in that awkward, staccato, interstitial space between words and real sentences, that often trails behind beauty like a wake, we all, for a mutually acknowledged moment, wondered what if. . . .

Desilicious

Sudden

VIKAS MENON

rain, a whiteghost,

streams mist
past a street lamp's
downcast eye.

My mind wanders.

Wind sprays
against a leaning elm,

its gnarled, brown bark:

a forehead's creased flesh,
the wrinkling at knuckle

a tongue licked down my chest.

Fall

VIKAS MENON

Northampton, Massachusetts–
while listening to Smt. Gangubai Hangal

At dusk we fall into her body
inside her dark jewel voice,
amber black blown glass.

Our muscles sore, teeth-marked
skin
and shaking fingers.

The cinnamon cream of your belly,
fluid sway
of shoulders pumpkin starred,

a bloodlunged throb below my navel.

Leaves deepen to crimson, autumn's skin.

I have fallen upon you –
a dry leaf moistened against earth,
borne by the wind,

fallen from branch.

Anoint

VIKAS MENON

Maybe the last time, I think
    tongue cleft thigh clutches jaw, head clasped
     fireflies flash behind lidded eyes
     moistloin coppersweat embrace
        thatch of hair abrades
       against tongue
faintsoap unbathed musk humid cedar
starkboned hips
   liquid tilt, muscleflow bellyquake,
    humbusting Again,
      your stomach lunges for air
   wet
      genuflect
      of flutterfinger
closes your eyes
        lips sprung and O and
        mouthing
          crimsonpale wall of thighs
        buffet my skull,
    your knees splayed, belly pearl

pinnacled,
   spine arched
  collapses
a salt shudder
 down throat
  burning my tongue,

its hangdog lap,
her silkbite

her clitlipped lick

Desilicious

Tuesday Night

NAVNEET ALANG

She has a network of tiny black hairs upon her back. They begin at the nape of her taut neck and work their way down in an almost invisible pattern to the soft flesh of her behind. An invisible web on her brown back, the hair and skin so similar that, under this light, you can hardly tell one from the other. And therein lies the beauty: the soft darkness, absorbing everything, drawing you into its warmth.

I trace them methodically with my fingers, playing, inventing cosmic patterns upon which we roam. Remarkably, she stays asleep, breathing quietly as the sun creeps its way across the room. The rising orb removes the quiet calm of dark and the effects of the night before – the mess, the bottles, the remnants of countless people pulsating through the house – the guilt – become clear. There is an odd smell in the air: perfume, beer, sweat, and sex; a strange combination, an odour that, if ever repeated, will evoke memories and conjure up images: of a throbbing crowd, wisps of blonde hair, and a great, gaping emptiness within me. Now that the bright light of the sun has arrived, however, the time for moments has passed. It is time to get up and put away last night, bury it deep within the earth, and pretend it had never happened.

I have been dreaming of this night for years. I have felt it, this bead, this diamond at the back of my brain, digging itself in, deeper. My big plan, the way to tie it all together, the hope to catch all the wild, flailing strings of other, greater lives and wind them into mine. There are snippets of everything that has ever touched me in this patched-together reel of film in my mind: the end of a Korn video, the beginning of a morning raga, the blonde tuft of pubic hair on a porn star – somehow these are all there, floating quietly in my mind, waiting expectantly for the chance to be played out on the fret board that is my life – a searing, distortion-laced jazz solo that ends in quiet, reverb-soaked plucks. And the dissonance – of the perfect picture in my brain and the vague impressions of the present is where I live and always will. There has never been a time where the pendulum has momentarily stopped on one side and I spend my life in a sincere search of moments of purity, like when a baby falls asleep in your arms or you realize how much you want to die. And I feel it now, have always felt it, throbbing ever so quietly like the artery you never notice, here in the decorations around the back garden; in the haphazard glow of the lights in the bushes that should have been my friends as a child. And she bustles around in her Type-A way, always carrying something and swinging her hips or showing off her smile capped by tinges of hair on either side of her upper lip.

I have this dream where I am always running: down a long, cold, snow-filled street, the kind that looks beautiful at Christmas. There is something behind me, chasing me, and I never know quite what, though once, inexplicably, it was Charlton Heston holding a rifle, and another time, as bafflingly, my father. I am yelling for help as I run, screaming at passers-by in between huge gasps for breath. They all turn their faces against the snow and against my calls as I watch the moisture from my breath disappear and vaporise into the frigid air. Shopkeepers slam doors shut, one-by-one, like a procession, like a fucking Thanksgiving Day parade. And with no escape, I keep running, endlessly.

"Rajeh, what do you think about putting the barbeque at the other end of the patio and setting up the three tables this way?"

"Yeah . . . sure, that makes sense. Hey, did you smoke a joint without me?"

I met Sonia at a local Indian take-out. In an attempt to duplicate sixteenth-century romances, my first words to her were, "Could I have three vegetarian *thalis*, please?" She replied as she would any other customer: "Of course, sir. Is this to go or would you like to stay here and eat?" She spoke to me in English, breathy but sharp. As she floated orders into the kitchen, she spoke Punjabi flawlessly, her eyes dancing in response to her inflection, moving back and forth between what were, to me, two entirely different worlds. Behind the counter, without so much as a blink, she was climbing my life's biggest wall in one swift, effortless motion. And instantly I had fallen.

Although I already considered myself an expert, I became quite the student of Punjabi food over the next few weeks. It didn't take her long to notice how frequent my need for a taste of home and casual conversation became – not to mention that she quickly picked up that home had far more to do with fish and chips than *saag-paneer*. Apparently she found my attempts to hide a puppy-dog affection under a veneer of dry, intellectual humour quite endearing – "Pathetic in a cute sort of way," was the way she would put it later.

Six months later, we had been dating for four and I felt that I had been saved from a life of intellectual destitution and emotional starvation. Up-tempo College Street coffee shop conversations where ideas ricocheted between us at a dangerous, unbridled pace, so quickly that we were radical neo-Marxists one night and conspicuous consumers the next. The words were merely empty vessels, though, vacuous ideas, containers for the intense and burning want. Whether or not Lorde's question about tools and houses had any relevancy in the Internet age were just curtains for the main stage brain fuck, some way that the point of satisfaction could be reached – Shit! You're just like me! – the intellectual fluids spilling everywhere. . . .

And in the middle of this, in this life lived for another soul, I ached and burned with the desperate need to bare mine. It began with late-night phone conversations that would end when the sun rose, then letters and hastily composed poetry. It's really incredible the things you can make rhyme with love. Then stories and songs dedicated to her, tapes made of myself speaking. Finally, one night I just broke down and only barely mouthed, "Thank you so much. . . ." She kissed my forehead, smiled, and got dressed. When she was ready to leave, she looked at me and said, "Grow the fuck up. You have so much more in you than this bullshit, so much more."

Winded by the sharp intake of breath like the shock from plugging in the old toaster oven with the wire bare, the dim kitchen lights brightening around me as the world grew suddenly real.

Two months later, I did what she asked: I grew the fuck up. When it was time, we held hands across a table at a coffee shop on Bloor and she said with a smirk: "*Tusi hoon bahaut siana hogiyah eh?*" We smiled and laughed and gently, quietly, fell in love.

But the moment GK gets the system hooked up, the vacant whispers and memories of my former self that bounce around in my head disappear. There is only the smooth, bubbling bass, the liquid evening air, and a talisman around my neck, taken from someone else and made mine. Clarity may be fleeting, but it is a beautiful thing while it's around.

The precious few who are here early run back and forth, throw Cheezies at each other and sneak in a toke before the crowds arrive. They invent new dances that allow them to express the dark fire inside while simultaneously carrying plastic bottles of pop and bowls of chips to the tables outside – careening like idiots across the patio, singing at the top of their lungs.

"Get out of the fucking way!"

"Shut up! She's not coming?!"

"No, dude, she is. And she's single!"

"Dude!"

"With his *girlfriend*?! Oh shit, why didn't you tell me! That's it, I'm going home, I'm going – no, *no*! I'm leaving."

"No, sweetie, sit down, sit down, it's okay, you can do this, you can deal with this. . . ."

"Rajeh, move the plates to the other end of the table."

And then I quickly pull her aside while the others are grabbing their precious beer from downstairs and steal a quick exploration of her mouth as my hands rest on the back of her thighs.

She smirks. "Sometimes I think I could tie strings around the electricity coming from your eyes."

"Hey, hey, I'm the poet of this relationship. Only *I* may say lines that."

"Yes, Professor –" she smiles. "Dumb ass!" A peck on the cheek and then back inside.

GK, our DJ for the night and a friend all the way back from Mr Kirkwood's English class, works at the grocery store down the street. He packs shelves full of fruits and vegetables whose names, flavours, and idiosyncrasies he knows and which have nothing to do with his education littered with titles like "Narratology in Ancient Greek Literature" and "The Constructions of Gender in the Work of Woolf." He does it well, with diligence and pride, not because he enjoys it, but because that's just the way he is. At the store, everyone calls GK "Gary." Management said that it would be easier for customers that way. His real name is Gurkirat and, from what he tells us, his Indian friends find his name-swapping dodgy at best. But we call him GK because as nice as Gurkirat is, GK makes more sense when you're in front of 2,000 dancing urbanites. Secretly, I know he is like me and resents us for it, wishing that his name "fit" everywhere and always.

But apparently, the identity complex looming in the background never comes. In the evenings, he deejays – spins, mixes, makes magic. For GK, just like the rest of us, what you do during the day is what you do to get by, because rent needs to be paid, because your '94 Civic just isn't "you" and because macaroni and cheese (despite its proponents) just doesn't cut it for dinner every day. So, you scrape by and you deal, with the all-employee meetings, with the cheers of success at the latest contract landed with the customers who only remember you as the dark-skinned fellow with facial hair and an accent. In reality, it's what you do in the comfort of night that counts, it's that which gives shape to the formless mass of your life. It is those meaningless moments spent staring into a clear but starless sky while cool summer air caresses your closed eyes that are real – fuck the job: it's what you do when you're off that counts.

But now, the evening crowd grows, slowly but steadily. It grows in movements, in philosophies, in histories. The university crowd arrives first. Then the clubbers. Then those who swear by the rave, and then those from high school you're so glad you kept in touch with. She has been here since morning, getting things ready, telling me that there will be plenty of time for loud music in the evening – and keeps hinting that there will be time for other things also. But you feel it hanging there – the disaster looming, the guilt at your prescience but with dogged determination to push on. And so you do, not knowing when the world will explode, cowering with a bright sunny smile for all the world to see.

It is early evening. The sun is beginning to set, and people I once knew as friends are turning into silhouettes that hold bottles and bob their heads. Four such ghosts crowd around in a circle and blue smoke wafts from between them. Others lose their human form altogether and turn into writhing shapes that somehow merge with the sound waves that hover in the air. The taste of tobacco and summer evening air is fresh on my tongue and a fragile feeling of contentment begins to build like a bomb in that spot in my mind that only music can reach.

John has a crowd around him. He's Sonia's friend from high school, and is one of those people who you wish you had gotten to know later on in life, when you knew more and weren't stuck like you are now.

Manmeet Alang

He stands ranting about the shift he works with at the plant. Sensing his growing success with the group around him, he plays the trump card, pulls up one pant-leg, kisses his teeth, and begins with, "I'm not a racist, but what the fuck is up with this?"

(But it's my garden. My moment. After the years spent thinking to myself after every little diatribe – "how can you be so fucking stupid?" – after every question about curry and its components, I fall prey to that which always looms around me. And there it goes, soaring like an albatross before me: my forearm, then my wrist, then four neatly arranged knuckles and then my humanity. And the soft thud-smack against pink skin and a quick couple of seconds later the world has become a storm of pain.)

The sound of a punch is nothing like it is in the movies, only an odd mix of wet and dry where one always overpowers the other, but is never consistently a winner. There is that prickly, gnawing tension in the air that bubbles up whenever the ubiquitous line of intimidation is crossed and violence splatters its red shards upon you. The feeling is unwelcome but not unexpected, wished away, but only like rain or humidity. It's part of life here, the old order and the new – or is it the new and the new? – clashing in a flurry of blows, with loud, wet-soft smacks.

No one knows how to react. There are those who move in by instinct, grabbing the flailing limbs, pushing the two suddenly faceless bodies apart. There are those who react in shock, those who are glad to see a fight. There is Sonia, who stands looking at a boy she no longer knows.

But nobody knows what to do with the anger hanging in the air – with my attempt at racial slurs that seem like empty threats. No one knows how to bring it back down, how to cut through the honey sheets now made opaque that would normally rest like diaphanous clouds over everything we breathe.

"Get out of my fucking yard." He stands perfectly still.

"What the fuck is your problem? I was just telling a fucking joke. I wasn't even near her. You could have just said something, but you, you fucking hit me and called me. . . ." He is bleeding. Good. His teeth don't look quite the way they did before.

"Get out of my fucking yard. Now." You stupid white trash, cracker fucking pale-faced, pasty-assed mother-fucki – "Leave. Now."

"Fuck you then, you. . . ."

But you can't hear the rest. Because of the anger. And guilt. Because you hate. Because you have become the root of all your pain. And the quiet smile that builds on the inside, like a happy cancer, when you remember the way it felt to finally smash your fist into its face. (Like a burst of joy wrapped in the sweetness of pure, malevolent rage.)

I wish I had an excuse for it. For the pain, for the emptiness within me; some great societal trend that declares, "I can't help it – it's everywhere!" But there is no Great War to come home from. There are no real revolutions overseas, or at least none that we know of. There is nothing – simply events that flash like lightning on screens. There is the brittle opening of Kurt's one and only song, the radioactive flash of a monitor, the thud-thud-thud from outside the club as scantily clad patrons shiver in the cold. Because, you have to just give up in the here and now and say fuck it, I'm gonna freeze my ass for half-an-hour, but I'll find a nice fella or gal inside to keep me warm until morning. I'm sorry, you'll have to forgive the constant switching of I and you – I keep forgetting.

But as the music smoothes out the bumps that make terror in the morning, the night, dark, black, and brown, deep like the colour of our skins, begins to roll over the city, spreads its warm, glowing fingers over the streets and blankets us in a cool, bubbling throb of anticipation.

And there, in the middle of all this, Pamela enters through the front door which is so undeniably hers. Tall and blonde and legs and eyes and white and spice and all of a sudden, the world begins to collapse around me, again. She is wearing a short black cocktail dress. And even if you try, you are lost in the curves of cleavage and thigh and the chime – I want – goes off in the back of your head and quite frankly who gives a fuck about women's lib right now when you just want a taste, are desperate for a piece of – . And you feel your tongue pushing against the back of your teeth as if somehow it wants to get out.

She wanders over, glides over as if floating, in a dreamy way, in whatever cliché helps you picture a temptress most clearly. She settles, wanders into the crowd, watches the subtle shifts and the invisible strings realign themselves to the new presence. And there, the spider is at the centre of the world's web.

My hands are clammy and cold against the back of Pamela's soft white thighs. I have already forgotten how things got here so quickly,

Navneet Alang

~ *91*

and I don't give a damn. Smiles, drinks, coincidence – what does it matter? In the bathroom upstairs, she is noisy, too noisy, all breath and muffled moans and shudders that scare me to my very core, for now they are mine. She smiles and turns serious, talks about the party, then is lost in the clenching of muscle, lightly tickles my nose with her hair down there and then giggles about how wet she is. She is like a walking dream, and I am the sleeper. It is me who enters, me who thrusts, and her who glides in tempo to my motion.

Finally, everyone has left. We – Sonia and I – make love, as if we are supposed to, as if it is expected. And it is. But it is tense and I swear that she knows. Is she writhing in pleasure or pushing me away? But still, I tell her, blurt out in a sentence while I am still inside her. She says nothing until we are finished. Until she is. The whole time spent staring directly into my eyes, never flinching once – as the image of her face moves closer, then further away, closer, then further away. And the enormous din of silence crushing all around me, radiating like dark into the centre of my blonde light.

I will spare you the agony of Sonia's tears and tantrums – not out of compassion for you, but because I never see them. She never lets me. In fact, I'm not sure there are any – I can only hope. She did relate one story, though: of a plate dropped while washing the dishes, of staring out the window into the sun, thinking of the time we rode off-road together for the first time and the beautiful crimson colour of my blood as it trickled down my shin, sparkling in the sunlight – but that was it.

It is morning and she awakes quietly. I am already up, thinking. She turns her enormous milk-bowl eyes towards me and smiles, vaguely. She mouths good morning, or at least I think she does. We spend the day in a subdued silence, a kind of Sunday quiet after a Saturday funeral. We are both supposed to be at work, but the question of going and the arguments as to why one shouldn't, never come up.

On another day she would have to convince me and entwine me in her wonderful words. She would condemn me for my conformity and reassure me that it's all a "self-reproducing system of practice and ideology, so my absence is simply a lull in my involuntary participation." Or she would just strip naked and stand there, leaning against the front door and ask – "Work or this?"

But today is different. There is something lacking in the air. A waiting. For time and minds to wrap themselves around deeds. To give life to the words. To give body to the hurt. To create sounds for the pain that cannot be spoken.

I don't know. We always talked about our place in the world. About how we were new and modern and how the great whitewashing system wasn't ever going to get us. And here we are. Close to tears, because the river that runs under everything has finally exploded over its banks into our lives. And yet, here we are, with the house left still standing. The world is looming dangerously close to our front door. But we are here.

And so she sits, across from me, at the kitchen table. The steam from the coffee drifts lazily upward and mingles with the pain and love that dangle in the air. I sit uncomfortably, awkwardly, as she stares deadpan, right into me.

"Why?"

"Because. . . . It haunted me my whole life."

"Now it will haunt me – both of us. Cut the poetry and stop fucking around. Why?"

"I don't know! Because it just simmers under my skin, because I finally *could*. . . ." She winces. "Because I wanted to feel alive . . . because . . . the night is so dark and so are you. . . ."

"I said stop fucking around! *Stop it!* How can you say things like that? Do you have any idea what this" – she points to her gut – "feels like? Speak English, you fuckin' asshole!" Her voice cracks with rage.

"Because, for fuck's sake! I finally felt alive." I cringe – so does she. But I can't hold back any longer. "Why . . . why don't you get that?" I feel guilty, horrible. I feel honest. "But it was like feeling a pulse for the first time. Because I live here and am sick and tired of denying it. This. Us! It's all about how we don't live here, about how we're different, about how we can live outside . . . whatever the fuck you want to call it . . . I wanted it. That's it. I desired. And so did she. For the same reasons, for the same fucking, stupid, human reasons . . . for the same. . . ."

It has been years, literally, since my cheeks were wet with tears of my own.

"What do you want me to say to that? *What do you want me to say?* Okay? Sure? No problem, I want to fuck a ripped white guy with a huge cock. Is that cool with you?"

"No! . . . no, you know. . . ." But finally, the space in my middle of my skull loses its foggy shrouds.

"Yes."

"What?! Wh –"

"That's what I need to know. That's what you need to know. You need to tell me that it's not just me. That, given the chance, you would do it too. That it's in the air we breathe."

"*What?* You want to hear *what?*"

Maybe there aren't words for what I want to say. Maybe there are and they have been said. But as soon as I speak, you feel something crack. Not the ground – reality isn't slipping away. But the shrouds around us. The soft, dewy honey in the air has hardened into crystal sheets, shattered, and now microscopic shards fall over the kitchen floor, silently, in the look of disbelief on the woman I now love more than ever.

It is the light of the dusk, perhaps. But as the dark approaches the room and casts a shadow upon her bare back, life unfolds itself in the darkness of her hair and skin. And I rest, my head pressed against the curve of the universe, my hand on the back of a leg, and her breath filling the entire cosmos. Pitch black, the stars are like painful pricks of light that make the otherwise warm glow cold and brittle. She turns, and I move, and she stares. And with a single look, unravels the greatest mystery of all. Takes my hand, places it against her lips, and we both fall, quietly, over the edge, into infinitude.

I don't think I can call what happened forgiveness. Instead, even in the beauty of her actions, to this day I still call it mutual guilt.

~

It is years later, but I have started to lose count. I sit cross-legged on the bed, staring at myself in the mirror that hangs over the dresser. Approaching my thirties, the thinning hair on my head is shaved short and there is a piece of steel awkwardly piercing my eyebrow, as if it were weakly saying, "Look at me."

The woman I love comes in, fresh from a shower, smelling of fruit. Dropping her towels, she wraps herself around me and drapes her long golden-yellow hair over my face and chest.

"I can't wait to meet your grandparents," she says softly. "I hope it's not too hot."

"Hot? Rajeh, I wasn't being silly: pack a jacket and plenty of warm clothes – northern India is cold in December."

"You mean you were serious? Oh, okay. . . ." She laughs. "I meant to say, you never give me a straight answer when I ask how well they speak English."

"'Cause I didn't want to freak you out ahead of time, and 'cause you should know. Why would farmers born in a village in the 1910s speak English? They never needed to, never had to, so they don't."

"What?!" she moans. "Oh, now I'll be a *complete* freak! It's bad enough I'm a *gori* carrying your child. Oh, now they'll hate me." She starts to wander about our cream-coloured bedroom, waving her arms and muttering to herself. Her sisters call this self-criticism the curse of her genius, and I agree.

The phone rings. She picks it up.

"Hello? Oh hey, you. How's it goin'?" I have waited so long for this casual warmth between them. "Sure, I'll get him for you."

"Udam sweetie, it's for you. It's Sonia."

As she hands me the phone, she mouths to me: *speak English!* She hates when I speak Punjabi to Sonia, because she feels left out. I know. That's why I do it. I can't explain it, but it makes me feel better. It assuages the quiet guilt that is forever nibbling and burning at the back of my head.

"*Hanji didi! Kidaaan?*"

"*Haan, main do haftian wich Chandigarh jaa riha han.*"

"*Yeah, mainoo eh jagga vee yaad ayagi, par uthey mainoo ziyada apnapan lagda hai te changa lagda hai.*".

"*Kee mutlab kyon? Tusi patha kyon —*"

"Here, my life is like a dream."

"And I'm always running."

Anarkali

MEHAROONA GHANI

Never before have I noticed my smell.

Copper red
pollen centre
soft bristles
here and there.

A spray of happiness
slight scented sweat
agarbatti, chamelli, gulab, hawa
blows through the bristles.

Perfume carried
from the fruit beneath my covers
tickled my nose
spread through my body.

Suddenly aware
filled with
subtle sensation.

Touched by mixed fragrances
awakened by my skin's sensual sweetness
I could
almost taste the juices
from the seeds of my core.

Payal

MEHAROONA GHANI

Waiting, I can see your bare ankles,
orange-hennaed fingers touch,
limbs, roundness, points,
space. You fill me.

Skin caresses smooth surfaces,
small bells, dulled silver renew with each step.
Rhythm in our song,
with distant *shennai* ambience.

Pleasure in a fast pace,
freedom.
Up and down your ankles,
intricate weaves jingle like
a chorus of orchestral triangles.

Left toe finds right ankle,
Adjusts my shapely body,
to a more pleasing position.

Continuing, I embrace you. Holding,
softness, tenderness, warmth.

Your hand shifts me,
rubbing the mark I have left
and a little
      drop
      of blood.

Sensation

MEHAROONA GHANI

Bombay lights blurred brightly
While passing by in an autorickshaw
From Dharavi to Boravili
Potholes filled the road.

Gas fumes mingled with dirt
Nose permeated with night air
Cough lingered at the throat
Soft sweat appeared
Along exposed midriff
Fingers explored.

Hindi melody flirted with the mind
Images of romance sequenced in dance
Kuch, kuch, hota hai
Every now and then
Red chiffon sari
Drenched in innocence.

Confessions of a Paki with Colonized Desire

or How Giving White Men Blowjobs Reproduces Colonialism

SHARMEEN KHAN

Out of the blackest part of my soul, across the zebra striping of my mind, surges this desire to be suddenly white.
– Franz Fanon, *Black Skin, White Masks*

In my many debates with my mother about marriage, she told me that getting together with a white man is very "typical." This is a sneaky strategy because she knows I always strive to be the freak of the group. But during our conversations, I can feel her fear: that I will choose a partnership with one of the blue-eyed devils she fears so much. And as I approach the age of twenty-five, my entire family is holding its collective breath to see if their Marxist-libertarian girl will shed the rhetoric of free love and accept her destiny of becoming the proper Muslim daughter with the rich Pakistani-doctor-husband.

It would be easy to say that since I grew up with white people, dating white men is a given. To be honest, I never really considered that I have only dated, flirted, loved, desired white men to be a problem. My thinking was, "Well, I'm turned on to who I'm turned on to. What to do?" And there's usually a huge diversity of them: skater boys, indie rock boys, writers, commies, activists, professors. But there are two main issues that affect my feelings of safety: their understanding of racism, and how they represent normalcy. And then I begin to wonder how neutral my desire really is.

One night I was going down on a white communist when it struck me. How possible is it to have "something" when racism is a reality between us? What kind of relationship is this? So from between his legs, I asked the question.

"Uh, what?" he moaned. "Come on, baby, don't stop."

"Wait. I'm serious. What goes on in your mind when I go on about white supremacy and racism?"

"Well, I think of how passionate you are," he replied, pushing my head down in a passive-aggressive way. "Like, you know, you're really beautiful that way. Your mind and desire to change the world." He then started pushing his hips up towards me.

I crawled up to face him. "I know this is a bad time, but I need to know how you feel. Do you feel implicated in any way? What do you see when we make out? What is going on in your head?"

"Well, to be honest," he replied curtly as he lost his erection (talking racism kills sex dead), "I never really think about it. I mean, I never considered you a woman of colour until you pointed it out that you were one. I am learning a lot, though. And I totally support all the stuff you do – like those workshops teaching people about racism and tolerance and stuff. But I really see us as equal."

He said it as though he thought I'd been waiting to hear those words for a long time: that when he uttered the words "we are equal," tears of happiness would well up in my eyes. At the thought of being equal. That gender and racialization don't exist. No power (except when he lets me tie him up). No issues. Just us.

Well, there were no violins in my head. I sat there and wondered why I was attracted to white men. Where does this desire come from? On the surface, it is easy to rant about racism and have them listen with as much sympathy and sensitivity they can muster. But in reality, it is impossible for them to understand. They try. They hold my hand and look empathetic. Or they'll say something like, "I can kind of understand because I've had bad stuff happen to me that wasn't racism. But close. Like *class-ism* [slowly enunciating it] because of, you know, my working class background." Or they were beat up by jocks in high school because they listened to bad British pop, or wore Doc Martens and eyeliner ("That's total discrimination, man"). Or their car insurance is higher because they're men. Seeing them try makes me smile. They're so tortured. But in reality, they don't see the world as I do:

1. "Fuck, we've been watching *Friends* for two years and I haven't seen one person of colour. What kind of New York City is this? A future New York where White Power has finally annihilated the brown folk?"

2. "I can't believe how fucked up *The Nutcracker* is! What's with the Oriental dance! Can you believe I wanted to be in this ballet as a child? We should phone in a threat next time it comes to town."

They usually do the "Relax, it's only entertainment" speech. But if I touch a nerve with a "Your punk scene/ revolutionary Communist Party/ protest/ group of friends/ entire ideology is *sooo* white," they roll their eyes and give me that look that says, "I don't mind talking about racism until you implicate me. So stop."

I have to say that in the past few years, I became sick of racism being my problem. That all the baggage around interracial dating became my problem alone. That I alone had to deal with confusion, self-doubt, and feelings of sadness keeping secrets away from the family – that it was always my problem. So slowly I have begun to voice it in the most intimate of situations. Calling them on their shit, bringing up their assumptions in the supermarket, over dinner, after sex. And I found it is the most difficult thing I can ever do, because it is one thing to do it at a rally or in a classroom, but with someone you are intimate with – there is a level of vulnerability that shakes me to the core.

This vulnerability comes from my need to be desired by white men. Those white boys – the way they carry themselves. The way they can concentrate on better things in life than racism or gender. The way they can make us brown girls feel white. The way they can make us feel just as worthy and sexy as white girls. It's an amazing talent. So I don't always mind when a man says that my skin is beautiful. That it excites him to see his white hand between my dark thighs. Because at least he finds me beautiful, even if I am the Other.

The weirdest situation is when you sleep with a guy who has only had white lovers, and you're his first brown girl – it's kind of like taking his colonial cherry. It's all up to you to be the first to introduce him to the wonderful world of racialized body image. You have to represent. You have to be gentle and loving, but forceful with the issues so that the pain and shame are momentary. Kind of like, "You are about to sleep with a girl who has wanted to be white for the majority of her life. You're sleeping with a girl who is projecting a lifetime of racism, a lifetime of hating brown and envying white. You are about to fuck around with my prison. It's a little different." And while it is a little uncomfortable to have sex with someone who doesn't love herself, you wonder what stereotypes he brings to the bedroom, if he notices that you are, indeed, not white, if he compares you to all of his white lovers, if it is exotic or if it's simply the coming together of two people – who live under a system of white supremacy – for the simplest desire of connection.

It's pretty shameful to admit it. And it's not a general narrative of my life. But I have to admit that my attraction to racialized men is mute. There's nothing. An empty cup. Some of it is because I grew up with white people. Some of it is because I hate my pigment and all those who share it.

And the difference in desire between men of colour dating white women and women of colour dating white men is a difference in power. The introduction of race and white supremacy leads to different stories and experiences for racialized folks trying to get love. The debate and contradictions between men and women of colour on sexuality, the Franz Fanon complex with white folk and how internalized racism impacts our relationships, is confusing and complex. Men of colour may bring their gender supremacy into heterosexual relationships, but have had lived experiences of racism that extend into and affect their desire. It is difficult for a woman of colour, myself, to fully comment on it because I bring a great deal of judgment and scrutiny to the discussion. But it is a discussion that I have been working on with my male friends of colour to figure out the links between racism and sexism. How they deal with the racism they face, but the privilege they have with their maleness and masculinity, and how that affects their relationships with white women (who benefit from white supremacy), and how we share similarities with desiring whiteness, but how that desire reproduces the gender roles that we are trying to overcome and how, then, their maleness is different from white men. For them, dating white women somehow comments or emphasizes their masculinity, while for me, dating white men reinforces roles of femininity, even though we all want to break it down and throw it out the window. See the difficulty?

The issue of desiring whiteness is not about "having" white men, but white men "having" me. Wanting me. For white men to desire me. Body image, self-hatred, and wanting to be desired are things that everyone deals with, but the impact and implications it has on different men and women are complex when race and Otherness come into play. And I have to say that as a feminist who organizes and believes in sisterhood, my relationship with white women is pretty fucked up. I am critical of them, I demonize them. I see a skinny, beautiful white girl walk by, and I picture a safe falling on her from the sky. It's hard to have solidarity with people you are jealous of – jealous of their normalcy, their representation, their power. Because I notice who white men and men of colour are attracted to. When I see my uncles marry white women or my guy friends with their skinny white girlfriends, I understand why. It's like watching a bad movie full of people who are beautiful, attractive, and normal.

Here is the problem: I don't fit normal beauty standards. Because brown girls can either be seen as totally exoticized or just plain weird. I haven't seen much in between. And this feeling of freakishness has stayed with me for a long time. Hatred over my skin colour. Hatred over my family's culture. Hatred over my religion. Something I tried to change at a young age when I read that drinking eight classes of lemon juice would lighten my pigment. Pretending to be Christian. Trying to lose weight. Trying to dress right.

Now, with the general neuroses of teenage years, race isn't a good additive. As one teacher described, there is no culture we racialized students can relate to, no culture we can join, no culture we can create, as we hang in limbo between wanting to be white and having a racialized identity. In such a state of mind, there is only one thing to do: go goth. And that is one thing I did.

And in high school, it was clear that white men didn't date women of colour. So when men approached me for unattached relations, I didn't really think twice. I thought, "This guy actually finds me attractive. I better use this chance while I can." High school was a period of bad body image, bad sex, and surrendering my power in relationship after relationship. Just because I felt that being with a white man raised me to a higher level.

In some sense, recounting all this pain is kind of funny. But for some reason, wanting to be white is more shameful than funny. There is something when a white man gives me the nod of approval, when he gives me thirty seconds of carnal attention. Asking to be respected, loved, and admired is too much. But to be fucked by a white man – that means I am not doing that badly.

And I have fallen in and out of love with so many of them. Even the good relationships when we listened and challenged each other on a regular basis. But once in a while, there are those moments when a white man falls asleep with his hand on my hip after a long debate about racism in our relationship, that I don't mind doing the work. Often, these issues can be left at the door when you can trust someone, acknowledge the gender and race powers, and make a commitment to each other to be honest about it with respect and dignity.

In other instances, whether it is a man who says that he loves my brown skin or that he doesn't see my skin colour, I shudder when his hands press my head down to his dick: exploring, conquering, and civilizing the dark land. The barbaric, uncontrolled areas. My dark nipples, my black hair. As his white hands move over every inch of my body, he slowly colonizes it. Since it has been graced by the white man, I can slowly assimilate. The belief that the more white men fuck me, the more I can be white. As if his penis is an instrument of infection. This is the problem of colonialism – the internalized racism and hatred over my own identity and wanting to be more like the colonizer. Even though there is shame and guilt, and a sense of defeat, a colonized mind is somewhat easier.

I figure that it's a little more work for a man to sleep with a woman of colour not because of the experiences of oppression and privilege that each brings to the bed, but because there have to be frequent discussions about the sexual ideology between women of colour and white men. To stop the cycle when women of colour feel that they need to work extra hard to prove themselves in order to be respected by white men. To talk openly about the politics of attraction, and to nip it in the bud before they create some weird post-colonial sexcapade in which their body represents the unknown, wild brown lands that need to be tamed by the white man's hands; in which the white man becomes the Colonizer – the all-knowing, all-guiding – in a parasitic relationship where the woman of colour does all the giving. No longer will I give up all of my resources, then feel grateful for the new railroad across my body. No longer will I reproduce notions of feminity that

Desilicious

make me the gracious South Asian housewife, happy for the scraps I get. It's a constant process of decolonization. To make it clear that an anti-racist framework must always exist intimately and in public. And that we must always remember the prison in the hearts and minds of those with histories in colonialism, imperialism, and plunder.

Sharmeen Khan

These Boots Are Made for Walkin'

SIDDARTH

"Hey dude, you wanna hook up tonight?" the tipsy, colourless white man in a fitted teal tank top said to me at the trashy side of the bar.

"What's the use," I said, innocently seductive, as I took a sip of my gin and tonic. "It's not like you could show me anything new."

"I could show you eight inches of raw passion that'll rock your world," he responded. He probably shoots his load as quickly as he said that, I thought to myself. Getting a little bored as he tooted his own horn about the nights of raw pleasure he had shared with "loads of dudes," I noticed the preppy guy on the other side of me take a nervous breath. He was an innocent-looking, clean-cut guy – the kind whose cheeks you want to pinch, but at the same time, whose ass you want to smack. Meanwhile, Mr Eight-Incher realized he wasn't going to have his way with me, so he stormed off, cursing something about the *Kama Sutra* being a piece of shit. If he could only comprehend the power. . . .

I casually directed my attention toward the innocent one. Dressed in khakis and a blue flannel shirt, he watched me out of the corner of his eye as I lifted my shirt ever so slightly to scratch my side, which gave him a chance to see the tender, brown skin I wanted him to yearn for. Wearing my '70s faded jeans and tight, blood-red shirt printed with a white picture of Shiva, I let out a sigh that I hoped he would notice.

"So . . . are you from L.A.?" he asked, his southern drawl timid and coy. I decided then, *I'm going to make him mine.*

"Yeah, been in L.A. since I was four," I replied, savouring the tip of straw as I watched him stare at my mouth. As much as I loved this, I couldn't ignore the pounding of the music on the dance floor as it called to its chutney queen. I motioned to the innocent one; he put his Long

Island ice tea down and followed me to the dance floor. I pushed my way through the club, littered with men and boys wearing everything from fitted tees to sweatshirts to little else but the glistening drops of sweat on their chests. Heads turned as they saw me stride confidently past them. I could feel their eyes undress me; under my breath I scoffed, *get some colour*. The music was even louder on the dance floor – it called to me, to the chutney queen, to dance divine. I took my throne on the floor with my new friend and began to move – all of my subjects turned to me and wished they were the ones I dragged behind me with the leash of seduction.

From Madonna to Mariah and from Amber to Avril, the heavenly melodies enticed my inner Britney-back-up-dancer to come alive. Twisting, turning, and bending, I entranced the innocent one to mad stages of sexual desire. Grinding against him, I could smell the vodka on his breath mixed seductively with the sweet scent of his musky cologne. Our eyes locked; I closed mine and envisioned where this might go. The door flings open and in burst two men: one pigmentless and the other sweetly caramelized, both passionately smiling and crazy with raw desire. The aroma of Delhi engulfs them as the *agarbati* burns into clouds of sandalwood. Clothes are ripped off bodies and tossed on the stairs, exposing supple nipples and torsos – desire begins to play her game. Licking necks, ears, foreheads, the two push back the turquoise saris draped across the entrance to the bedroom. The seducing desi lets the *gora* think he is in control; little does he know. The colourless man, a tattoo of a dolphin on his left scapula, leads the other to the bed. The apartment is silent except for their heavy gasps for air. As they come upon their lair of love, they pass the altar decorated with silk screens of *Devis* and *Devtas*. Kali gives them a deceptive wink as they descend upon the black silk sheets. . . .

I opened my eyes in a cold sweat and realized that seducing a white man was easier than taking candy from a napping babe. They took my land and deserved to pay for it, so I'd make them beg . . . plead before they could reach my Promised Land. I quickly regained my composure, removed his hand from my belt buckle, turned around smiling sweetly, and said, "Thanks for the dance, I'm done."

I turned away, swayed my hips to the sound of Janet (Ms Jackson, if you're nasty), and was then pulled into a dance circle of five masculine white men looking for some brown sugar. But they needed to look elsewhere as I checked them out up and down, chuckled, and walked away. It was then that I saw him. He was in the corner of the club freaking some unattractive guy in chinos. He was like a chocolate delight: clearly desi in his "I Heart India" tee, I could almost smell the jasmine soap he used, taste the remnants of chai on his lips. He glanced at me and then, ever so carefully, pushed the man, who was at this time raping his neck, away from him. I don't remember the song or anyone around us at that time; as far as I was concerned, the two of us were the only ones there. Like Indian deities coming together, we started dancing in each other's direction. His gyrating hips moved in sync with mine. His hazel eyes were set upon me as we inched our way to each other. In classic Indian style, we tried to out-dance the other with crazy hip and leg movements. From kicks to booty shakes, we danced, eyes locked on each other for what seemed like forever. Finally, when we both recognized we danced as well as the other, we cautiously approached one another, our open palms anxiously waiting the arrival of the other's.

Then it happened. The touch – like fire to fire. Not like an electric connection, but like a completely incompatible sensation, we immediately became revolted. Our eyes lost the connection and we quickly turned away from each other, looking back and understanding it was never meant to be – brown on brown can just never happen. Walking away from my desi counterpart, I felt an emptiness inside of me. It's not like I've never met queer desis, but it would have been refreshing to meet one who mirrored my style – knowing the power I hold over white queer men because of my ethnicity and colour and how I can exert that power and use it to tease them. Just as I was coming to the harsh realizations of the evening, Mr Eight-Incher, who had so benevolently decided to forgive me for being a prick to him earlier, wanted to take me for a ride I'd never forget. Smirking confidently, I responded, "Nice try, but I have some standards."

It's a familiar story: white man meets brown boy, white man smiles, brown boy kneels, white man's head rolls back. Well, I'm not your normal brown boy. I'm sick of being the "curry whore" whose spices are free for the taking by bland mouths. At the same time, as I am sexualized, I am also ignored – a classic case of the colonial double standard usually reserved for white men and women. Though I am "colourly restricted," in the gay world, I seduce white men into the same position they stereotypically place people of my colour. In my world, here's how the story ends: brown boy smiles, white man kneels.

Welcome to my Empire – leave your self-respect at the door.

Siddarth

The Darker the Berry

GILES PINTO

My sex life has been a fraud. I'll tell you why: for most of it, the women I've been involved with have seen me not as a handsome Brown practitioner of the Tantric arts (which I am) but rather as a well-endowed Black stud (which I'm not). It's not my intention here to debate the mystique which surrounds men of African descent within the global zeitgeist. My objective is simply to come clean – no pun intended – in the eyes of those who may appreciate what I've been through. And what I went through is symbolic of the South Asian experience in North America; until recently, we were an invisible minority and we often found ourselves absorbed by the very visible minorities surrounding us.

For me, it all started in grade four, when I met my friend S. We were living in Saudi Arabia, within a walled compound that functioned pretty much like a Little America – right down to the racist attitudes which percolated under the surface of society. S. was Black and beautiful, showing up on the first day of school in a beret and bell bottoms, out-styling the rest of us guys from the get-go. He took a liking to me, saying that us "coloured people" needed to stick together. Over the next several years, I grew up in his shadow – imitating his speech, his manner, his dress. I saw early on that even though many of our peers disliked him (especially the males), many others adored him (particularly the females). And I let some of that teenage sex appeal rub off on me, hoping to "pull the honeys" with as much ease as he did.

I realize now that S. was a kind of revolutionary. In our privileged expatriate world, he could do things pretty well unthinkable back in the U.S. – such as seducing K.C., the blonde-haired daughter of a former Marine and a future prom queen. When S. returned to the States a year before graduation, K.C. became my girlfriend. She did it without much fanfare, selecting me casually out of the many heavy-breathing, sweaty-palmed candidates early in the school year; from the moment I received the good news from her emissary, a member of her inner circle, I found myself wondering in amazement at my good fortune. I wasn't Black like S., but I was Brown – which apparently seemed sufficient in her eyes.

During the next several months, as my hormones raged, I managed to "round the bases" with the girl universally acknowledged to be the most beautiful in our school. She was as pure as I imagined snow to be, and I felt somewhat guilty for defiling that image. But while I copped a feel or got into some serious necking, I always remembered the lessons I had learned from S., when he would recount his exploits with K.C. and his other compound conquests. If it gave her some kind of perverse thrill to make out with someone who resembled the local gardener, who was I to complain? She was too sweet and kind to ever say such a thing, but I'm fairly certain it crossed her mind at least once as I was struggling to undo her brassiere. . . .

A year later, after we moved to Canada, things became even stranger for me with regard to the opposite sex. In the small prairie town where we settled, I was labelled as "Black" from the moment I set foot in the high school. By a kind of redneck logic, if I wasn't white or Native, then I had to be Black. Of course, it didn't help matters that I loved to play basketball – or that I cruised around the community's gravel roads with rap music blaring from the speakers of my mom's car. And I must admit that my newfound exoticness ensured that I got to know a fair number of the local girls quite intimately, very often in the back seat of that same car. But I did try in vain to convince my friends that some substantial ethnic differences existed between me and, say, Michael Jordan.

By the time I entered university, I thought the jig would be up. Yet for the first few years, I continued my deceiving ways, seducing farm girls who wanted to be physiotherapists and small town beauties destined to become teachers. If they ever felt disappointed that I didn't quite measure up to the phallic standards popularly ascribed to Black men, they never showed it. I like to think this was because of my skill between the sheets, but I now know that women often conceal their concerns in the bedroom – especially when the lights are out. I finally met my match in a diminutive Bengali-Canadian engineering student, who liked me not for what I was but rather for what I wasn't: I imagine

Giles Pinto

I was the most laid-back and westernized Brown guy she had ever encountered. Unfortunately, I had to end the relationship when I was offered a job teaching English in Japan.

When I arrived in the Land of the Rising Sun, the first person I met was D., an Eritrean refugee who now called Ottawa home – and who had been assigned to work in the same town as me. He and I wandered through Tokyo's entertainment district, marveling at all the Africans employed for the sole purpose of luring people walking by into their respective nightclubs. The next day, during a break in our official orientation, someone told us that many Japanese girls had started seeking out Black boyfriends since there wasn't as much shock value in having a white consort in the clubs. Over the next three years, watching D. get accosted on the street and even in his apartment by lustful Japanese women, I felt an unbelievable sense of *déjà vu*. Sure enough, that old Black magic spread to me as well – but, of course, not to the same degree. What surprised me the most about this whole set-up was that D.'s strange magnetism applied equally well to many of our fellow teachers, a majority of whom were white and away from home for the first time in their lives.

The only group unaffected by his charms were a small contingent of Black women, who seemed to have seen it all and come out the other side with the scars to show for it. They especially intrigued me because they saw straight through my little charade, which had brought me so much success for most of my sexual life. I found their cool disdain unbelievably attractive. A few years after I returned to Canada, I met a woman who, for the first time in a long time, saw me as I was. I had just been "disengaged" from another all-American girl who had been drawn to my dark juju, but who couldn't handle the confused desi who came with it. Now, as I lie in the arms of my West Indian goddess, she playfully calls me "babu" and jokes about how much darker I need to get. I couldn't tell you what the future holds for our relationship, but I do know that I'm done pretending to be someone I'm not.

From Promiscuity to Celibacy: A Creative Piece on Sexuality

SHEILA JAMES

I am a South Asian slut. Raised a dutiful daughter of Indian immigrant medical doctors, I realized early in life that I would fail to meet the professional and personal expectations of my parents. You see, I aspire to nothing more than to have a good . . . no, a great, sex life.

My obsession with sex began when I discovered the "dirty" pictures in the *National Geographic* magazines (you know the ones). I would take them to my room and greedily devour them with my six-year-old eyes. Often I'd share them with my friends, wondering if they too felt those exciting tingles at seeing full breasts and the dark nipples of the African woman. I dreamt that one day my breasts would emerge so dark and full, but that dream has yet to reach fruition. My penchant for *National Geographic* came to a halt, though, when I was caught red-handed by my shocked and disappointed mother. "Shameful girl" echoes over and over in my head and the magazines were moved to my parents' office. This incident, however, didn't dissuade me one bit. By putting pen to paper, I realized that I could create my own anatomically correct characters. Pictures of naked bodies surfaced all over our house: on the telephone directory, in my sister's scribblers, on desktops and walls. My art, of course, was quite naïve. You see, I knew little about sex and even less about sexual intercourse. It was not until I discovered the *Kama Sutra* in my parents' bedside table drawer that the world of fucking was opened to me. . . . Was it 69 or 169 positions? I examined each drawing one by one, imagining my perfect, puritanical parents engaging in such activity. Well, well, well. . . . With their unspoken go-ahead, my fantasies flourished.

I entered my own fantasies as a super sex star. Naturally, I became well-endowed. Unnaturally, I became a blonde. Why not? All the sex objects on TV and in films and magazines were blond-haired and blue-eyed. I figured I could adjust the colour in my head to fit the role. Who would ever know? As my fantasies became more detailed, I sought new inspiration. Where else could I find detail but in my parents' medical journals. This is where I first glimpsed the female genitalia. As non-traditional casting was not yet in vogue, all the photography models were white-skinned. I saw pink vaginas, pink lips, white assholes. "Hmmm . . . so this is what it looks like," I thought. I decided a self-examination was long overdue. You can imagine my surprise when, at the age of nine, I squatted over a small hand mirror to discover that my hot pink vagina was modestly covered by purplish lips, and leering at me from behind was the wrinkly eye of my little brown asshole. It was mocking me, saying, "Ha ha, we fooled you!" Did I really think that my genitals would resemble the ones in the photos? Talk about internalized racism.

The years went by and puberty hit. Pimples, strange proportions, and other teenage problems took me under . . . to the world of my fantasies. I had thousands of scenarios featuring different people, different places, and different positions. One of my favourites was the fantasy in which I became a high-class hooker. Of course, I knew nothing about the reality of prostitution. I simply associated the profession with lots of sex, which I wanted, and lots of money, which I also wanted. Luckily for my parents, I didn't take my vocational dream too seriously. Problem was, I was bad in business. I ended up sleeping with people for free! Well . . . not exactly free. There are always small paybacks. Like flattery, for instance. I discovered very quickly that the fewer clothes I wore, the more compliments I'd receive. It got so that I'd be on a date, stark naked, saying, "Ah, gee you don't mean it. Ah, go on. . . ." I guess I should add that I experienced my first date, first kiss, and first lay all in the same night. I was nineteen, in university, and extremely horny. You see, being a South Asian girl living in a predominantly white, middle-class town and having a curfew at eight-thirty minimized my chances of getting many dates, let alone a boyfriend. But don't feel sorry for me. My early twenties proved quite active.

Sex soon became a substitute for everything: food, drugs, exercise, recreation, attention, affection, and unfortunately, love. It was a big ego booster and I shared my ego with everyone. Yes, I've been around the block enough times to know the neighbourhood. And the drivers have been of both sexes. No, gender was never an issue. I lusted after men and I lusted after women, so please indulge a little generalization: my experience has shown me that men are easier lays than women. Put it this way: I've slept with most of my male friends and tried to sleep with most of my female friends. Ah, but this shouldn't come as a surprise in such an outwardly heterosexual and heterosexist world.

Some friends say I should identify myself as bisexual, but I'd rather just call myself sexual. After all, I do have sex with myself and I must admit that I am the most willing, reliable, and faithful partner I've ever had. Fifteen years and the flame still burns. Of course, sex toys help: dildos, erotic literature, the old hand mirror. On nights of self-absorbed passion, I often hold the mirror above my vulva pretending I am my own lusty lover. What a change from the medical journal days.

Yes, a lot of things have changed. I decided to commit myself to a year of celibacy. During this time, I reflected upon my sexual history and how it was somehow shaped by the images in the environment around me. I had internalized racism and sexism to such a degree that my way of belonging was to be sexually acceptable to almost anyone. My needs propelled me down a reckless road. There was both fun and frustration along the way but most of the time I felt I had lost control of the wheel. The year of celibacy not only helped me to develop amazing self-control, but self-satisfaction as well. After lots of gentle caressing and self-discipline, I've come to love my cunt. Now I see sexuality as a jewel: sometimes undervalued and given away, other times over-controlled and locked up, and all too often forced from us against our will. In some hands, the jewel is dull. In other hands, it emanates light and beauty. But as long as it remains in the right hands – mine – it works like a gem.

My Spicy "Wagina"

MEHNAZ SAHIBZADA

The first time I heard the word *vagina* was in my seventh-grade biology class. Sex education was the topic and all of us school kids were squirming in our seats with excitement and embarrassment as the teacher explained reproduction. It was there amidst a chaos of words like copulation and procreation and ovulation that "vagina" first fell upon my ears. Until then, as crazy as it sounds, I simply had not heard the word. I knew I had one, but it was my "pishy" place. Put blatantly, folks, my brown lips were a pee tunnel, a place that only came to mind in the bathroom. After that biology class, I would think of vagina clinically for years. Dangling somewhere between "pishy" place and science, it would take me several moon cycles before I ventured between the deep dark folds to experience an orgasm and taste the glistening sweetness of my wet chutney.

My family is originally from Pakistan, and they immigrated to America in the 1970s when I was a baby with a baby vagina. I grew up in L.A., and at home my parents never once mentioned the word to either me or my sister. In fact, we operated as though thoughts of sex and body parts didn't exist. They were simply not a part of the human experience. If someone blurted out the word "sex" by mistake, one would think it was a fobbish pronunciation of the number six. And if my parents had said the word "vagina," it would have been pronounced "wagina." I'm so convinced of this pronunciation that every time I see my naked body in the mirror the word "wagina" intuitively pops into my mind. I picture my parents in matching green *shalvar kamizeezes* dancing arm in arm and singing the word over and over again in unison. It's very disturbing. They're smiling so broadly I think of Lucy and Ethel on *I Love Lucy*. It's at this point I consider going back into therapy.

But it's not *entirely* their fault. I was a prude since birth, one of those annoying good girls who loves everything and everybody. If a kid hit me on the school playground, I'd say, "I'm sorry." If a friend asked my opinion on her atrocious new haircut, I'd say, "You look fantastic." If an aunty told me I'd gained weight, I'd laugh as if she'd just delivered a compliment. Such has been my weakness. People call the monthly bleed "the curse." For me, the curse has been over-niceness. In high school, if my towel accidentally brushed against my genitals while drying my body after a shower, I'd say, "Excuse me."

As you can see, I was bound to be a late bloomer.

Bloom I did, however. I've recently come to love my brown, wet, slimy, and spicy vagina. Yes! Masala her up with a little cumin and turmeric and *vah!* She tastes divine. My husband tells me so.

As a teenager, I never poked or prodded my vagina, and the few boys I was intimate with were never offered admission. I would have made a good usher at a movie theatre, preventing kids from going into R-rated movies. Anyway, I just didn't understand fingering, and to be honest I still don't. My vagina was where I peed, or so I thought quite ignorantly. It never occurred to me to stick a finger there to find my clit. If only I knew I had the power to get myself off!

My first masturbation experience – I mean, first serious, non-prudish attempt – occurred during my junior year in college. By this time most men are masturbation gurus, but I was just beginning. I had recently read about the joys of masturbation in some sex book and had started dating a guy I liked very much. And I wanted to howl. To experience the big "o." To make my "wagina" scream "*vah!*" So I thought it was time for some practical exploration. I decided to try one night on my bed in a house I rented with two other students. I closed the door to my bedroom, turned off the lights, lit a candle, and put on a Sade CD. I threw on a white silk night shirt and a pair of black high heels. (Yes, I was a cliché waiting to happen.) I got into my twin-size bed. I had just taken a shower and had smothered my body with some heavily perfumed and cheap lotion, but this started an allergic reaction. So I had to pause and blow my nose, which could have ruined the perfect and supposed sophistication of the moment, but I didn't let it. Then I finally lay back and read some erotica. When I was sufficiently aroused, I tossed the book aside and slid a nervous hand down my stomach, past my pelvis, and between my legs. I had the urge to laugh but suppressed it. I stroked my hair then dipped between my lips where it was wet and warm. I tried poking around for a few minutes but couldn't get a vibe going. Instead of "*vah!*" I shouted "yuk!" It was slimy and gross. I got distracted and irritable. The sexual fantasy I'd been nurturing in my mind began to fade. Suddenly my mom's big serious head popped into my head:

"Don't play with your 'wagina'!" she yelled.

"Go away!" I screamed.

"You dirty girl!" my mother retorted.

Then my dad's smiling face appeared. "Vhat's going on, *baitay?*" he asked cheerfully.

"Shit!" my mind howled. "Nothing, Dad," I muttered aloud to the empty room, throwing a blanket over my half-naked body.

That was it. The moment was ruined and I couldn't continue. I turned on my side in frustration and faced the room. My eyes fell onto the small book shelf near the bed. The spine of my small Qu'ran stuck out at me and then came the guilt and weirdness about wanting to play with myself. "God must masturbate," I said out loud. "Does God have a vagina?" I continued. "Does she shave it? Does hers smell like seashells? Does God own a silk negligee and thong underwear? Does she?!"

Finally I pulled myself together. "Some things are better left unasked," a saner part of me advised.

I got up, changed into sweats, and went looking for some ice cream. And that was that.

~

The big "o" did eventually come for me, however, but the first time wasn't through masturbation. My boyfriend was over one night and we were messing around in my bedroom listening to the Cranberries. He went down my body, tracing me with small tender kisses. He started with my lips, then my neck, breasts, stomach, and before I knew it, he was between my legs, his tongue gently tracing the raw flesh of my vagina. I'd never let anyone do that before.

"What are you doing down there?" I squirmed. I was embarrassed yet curious. It was like being back in my seventh-grade biology class, knowing the subject at hand was of interest, but there was something wrong about enjoying it. But here I was, an unmarried desi woman, lying on a bed with my white boyfriend who was about to deliver the first taste of divine pleasure I had never dared experienced. His tongue continued to trace my vagina and soon my tense legs began to relax. *How can he like this?* I thought to myself. *It's so smelly . . . so gross . . . so brown . . . and it's a "wagina"!*

"Hush!" the desi diva in me whispered. I submitted and my legs relaxed. And, oooooh baby, did I relax. And then I knew it was going to happen. I felt the wildness, the irresistible dirtiness, the divine freeness of my weightless legs, parted from east to west for my man, yes, but more for me. Then the sirens began to ring and the room began to spin and I was there, sitting in a first-class seat on an airplane, sipping a martini, and twirling in the midst of my *big fat* "o"! And I knew when I screamed, "Oh my God!" that this *really* was a sacred experience. I thought of my book shelf, the Qu'ran still nearby, and I knew God wanted me to have this orgasm because God is a woman and her orgasm is a form of prayer. So I was going to let my man lick my spicy "wagina" while I thought of the turmeric and cumin swimming in my rich brown blood.

Ummmmmmmmmm!

Yessssssssssssssss!

Please don't stop!

Vah!

I let out a scream. It was more a cry of pleasure than a scream. My vagina was on fire and the fire had burned my guilt and liberated me. Then, for the first time in my life, my vagina began to sing, and this is what came out:

. . . *pehli pehli baar dehkha ahisa jalva*

Hoi! ahisa jalva

yeh larki hain ya shola

yeh larki hain ya shola. . . .

~

Afterwards, while my man held me, how I laughed and cried and laughed. I thought of the emptiness of my orgasmless past in the swell of the years behind me. And I thought of the spread of years to come, full of sweet pleasures and unexpected *silsilas*. And yes, I do masturbate now, and I know how to make myself come. It's a sacred ritual I practice, an essential part of my worship. And I think of the word "wagina" less as a derogatory mark of my flawed heritage, or my fobbish parents, but as a celebration of my own spicy brown skin. The word "wagina" is a sound and the sound is a river and the river is a gift. And my gift is the proud, strong, beautiful, and searching women in my life, from both the east and west, who celebrate the importance of the sacred "o" as their sexual richness and the cosmic circle of all womankind. We deserve pleasure. It's what makes us whole, come full circle: the multicultural, cosmic "o."

Mount Lemon, Chutney Style

MEHNAZ SAHIBZADA

what is it about a white hand
on a brown breast
that screams dirty

here in the land of
hamburgers and milkshakes,
highways and rest-stops,
players and whores, my mind traces
the possibilities of two mismatched bodies
making love in the woods,
small sharp twigs cutting into bare backs
and the background music – something
1980s bollywood – echoing off the trees

the misplaced white romeo, an awkward
substitute for *amitab*, and I the unlikely muslim
rekha, trying not to picture my mom cooking
aloo palak while my dad watches wheel of
fortune on the large screen color tv at
home in los angeles, both
of them quite sure i'm studying math
in my dorm room in tucson

at the age of eight i planned on
marrying some desi filmy hot-shot
and wearing bright mango-coloured saris to greet him
every evening when he got back from work,
at night he'd rub olive oil on my shoulders
and i'd giggle and look away when his

hands reached to unzip, then we'd break into song

instead i feel an anglo hand pushing into
faded blue jeans, nudging me into
a white chocolate fantasy,
silsila turned inter-racial sizzle

Desilicious

Desi Families

NISHANT VAJPAYEE

JYOTI

Jyoti kept her palms on the long, baggy pants she had changed into from her circulation-stopping flared jeans just before last period at school earlier today. They were sweating but with a rub or two became inconspicuously dry by the time she had to raise her plate of *puri*'s and *saag paneer* to her mother, who was ladling *chole* into the empty, small steel bowls on everyone's plate. From fear and experience, Jyoti had become an expert at hiding her nervousness when she had to lie to her parents in order to go out on dates. After all, if her father had even a hint of suspicion when she asked for permission to go out with her friends, he'd instantly say no. The usually annoying dimmed chandelier – her father didn't like too much brightness after spending the whole day seeing patients at his clinic under bright fluorescent bulbs – calmed Jyoti as she spoke up.

"Papa, Shezeen asked if I could spend the night at her house next Friday," she said quietly in Punjabi. "I told her no at first, but she kept asking me over and over again and said why can't I spend the night at her house when I sleep over at Nandini's house all the time. So I told her I'd ask you."

Jyoti's father sat at the head of the long, cherrywood dining table. He continued to eat but lifted his eyes and stared at Jyoti for some time while she held her breath in torturous anticipation.

Ever since he had immigrated to Canada, Jyoti's father had always been busy with work. He had worked as a cashier all day and studied nights for his medical board exams when Jyoti was a newborn, had slept during the day and worked night shifts at the only hospital willing to hire him when she was in elementary school, and now that he had established his own practice, worked long hours and spent evenings absorbed with reviewing charts and completing paperwork since Jyoti had begun high school.

Growing up, his life had been driven by his own father, who had simply told him to spend all his time studying, to apply to medical school, to apply to foreign residency programs, and had told him who to marry. As for anything other than academics and marriage, Jyoti's grandfather raised his son by example, by commenting on the rights and wrongs of other families and their children, and comparing Jyoti's father to the bad seeds when a lesson was needed. Jyoti's father, it seemed, had never questioned his parents' directives. Why would he? They had led him to a life more successful and fulfilling than he could have even dreamed on his own.

And though Jyoti's father realized that this new country and culture required adjustment of the tried and true methods of his own father, as his time became more and more devoted to succeeding professionally, he simply fell back on what was familiar when raising Jyoti and her brother.

"Tell her you have to go to the *mandir* that evening," he replied curtly, also in Punjabi.

"But Papa, I want to go. Why can't I? She's my best friend, and I feel bad for saying I can't go over every time she invites me to spend the night," Jyoti said, still sounding obedient.

Jyoti's father had been more lenient with his daughter when she was younger. However, a few months after he had established his medical clinic, he was visited by a girl from Jyoti's middle school. She had been pregnant. Since then, he spent the little time he had with Jyoti making sure she was focused on her schoolwork (at which she didn't seem to be excelling), that her clothes weren't too risqué, that her friends were limited to the daughters of Indian parents from his background whom he knew well and who held the same values as him, and, most of all, that any access to a secret boyfriend was completely out of the question.

"Why do you need to go to her house for the night? You already go there after school. What are you going to get from staying there for the whole night? They eat beef, you know that. You want to eat from the same knives and forks that have had beef on them? No, there's no reason for you to go over to her house and sleep. You can go there after school one or two days, and that's enough." He called into the kitchen to his wife to bring some water.

"Papa, it's just something girls do here. We're not doing anything wrong, just sleeping over. We stay up late and watch movies and talk. It's fun, Papa. If I'm not doing anything wrong, why can't I have friends like everyone else?" Jyoti was modulating her voice to make it crack, showing that she was near tears. She expected her mother to chime in soon for a final big push. She had prepped her mother with a guilt trip before her father had come home, implying that Shehzeen was sad because she thought Jyoti's mother and father hated her for being Muslim (pretty much true, but even her parents thought it wrong to make it known).

"Jyoti, I just don't see what's so fun about sleeping in someone else's house," her father said less rigidly, easing his approach in light of his daughter's seemingly passionate entreaties. "You don't have your things there; you'll have to sleep on the floor or in dirty sheets; you won't have a proper dinner. Why do all that? No. You can go to Nandini's house if you want, but not hers."

The day he had come home from the clinic after telling Jyoti's fifteen-year-old classmate she was pregnant and needed to talk to her parents (to which the girl had snorted a laugh through her tears), Jyoti's father closely watched his barefooted daughter as she washed the dishes. She had the body of a woman. He noticed her breasts, still alert with youth, their womanly suppleness visible through the tightly stretched T-shirt, and the bit of her slim muscular stomach and long back that peeked out from beneath the knot she had tied at the bottom of the shirt. Her long slender legs ran from the hem of her shorts that barely and tightly covered her behind. He looked at her until she finally turned around and said, "Hi, Papa!" with a wide smile. That night in bed, he firmly scolded his wife for allowing Jyoti to wear such clothes at her age. "Don't you know how to raise a daughter? Did your father let you wear such things?"

Jyoti sensed an opening now that her father was asking questions rather than giving mandates. "So since I can go to Nandini's but I can't go to Shehzeen's, it pretty much *is* because she's Muslim, right? If that's what it is, Papa, just say it so that I know that I can't have Muslim friends."

Jyoti's father always felt uncomfortable when he had to face his own discrimination, given that he had been on the misfortunate end of it himself for so long early in his career. "It's not that, Jyoti," he said, embarrassed and aggravated by his daughter's protest. "Have I ever told you not to go to her house?"

"Yes! You said that the first time I asked!" Jyoti said, excited at catching her father's mistake.

"That was because I didn't know her!" her father yelled, getting more upset. "Don't try to be smart with me, Jyoti. I said no and that's final!" Jyoti then burst into tears.

As always, her father began to feel remorseful. "*Dekh*, it's not that I don't like Muslims or anything like that. It's that their culture is different, and you won't be comfortable there."

"But Papa, I *do* feel comfortable! Aunty and Uncle are *so* nice to me, and they treat me just like they do Shehzeen," Jyoti said, sniffing through her tears, trying to make her father feel even guiltier for disliking people who treated his daughter so well.

"Why not let her go?" Jyoti's mother finally said after she'd brought out freshly made mango *lassi* for her husband. She held Jyoti's head in her arms, quieting her. "She's not doing anything wrong. Girls need to have time with their friends too." Despite his earlier proclamation, Jyoti's mother could see that her husband was on the fence and would view her speaking up not as defiance but as advice.

Jyoti's father sat silent with a worried look on his face. "I still don't know why you want to go. I don't want you spending every weekend there now, okay?"

Jyoti looked up, sensing a change of heart. "I just want to go this one time, Papa. It's already the end of senior year. I don't know if I'll even see Shehzeen anymore."

"Give Mummy your number. And I don't want you leaving her house after dark, do you understand?" her father said in a serious tone.

"I won't, Papa. Her parents don't even let *her* leave the house after dark," she lied. Shehzeen's curfew was ten on weekdays, eleven-thirty on the weekends.

"And I want you back in the morning, first thing after you wake up." His brows were still furrowed as he stared at his daughter, looking for any glint of deception in her eyes.

"Okay, Papa," she said.

He looked at Jyoti closely and then her mother. "*Acha*, go then," he said, turning back to his dinner. Jyoti's mother patted her on the head and finally sat down to eat.

Jyoti's heart raced with exhilaration, but she calmly tore off a small piece of her *puri* and scooped up some *chole* and ate. She knew it had gone far too smoothly when her brother, grinning, said, "Hey, isn't next Friday prom?"

Jyoti didn't flinch. She kept on eating while her father turned his gaze back to her. She chewed slowly while her mind raced to find something safe to say. In a moment of genius, she landed on an alibi that perfectly played upon her parents' preconceived notions.

"Yeah, it is. That's why me and Shehzeen want to hang out together. She can't go either because dancing and music is *haram*, so her parents aren't letting her leave the house that night, either." She waited with her heart in her throat until she noticed her father's look of satisfaction as he finished his *lassi*. She gave her brother a menacing stare as he giggled, and finished her dinner in an uncomfortable mix of euphoria and false composure.

Jyoti couldn't wait to call Shehzeen after she finished washing the dishes.

"*Gudia?*" Her mother whispered her nickname, meaning "doll," in her ear. "You and Shehzeen *are* just having a sleepover, right? Don't make me look like a fool for taking your side." During her entire married life, Jyoti's mother had only been able to get her way by playing on her helplessness. She knew that even this small power would be greatly diminished if she ever pleaded for a decision that turned out to be wrong. In fact, she came to Jyoti more for her own sake than out of worry that her daughter may not actually be spending the night at her friend's house.

"Of course, Mummy, Shehzeen can't even go out after dark. We're going to be in all night. You can call her house whenever you want to check up on us."

Jyoti's mother smiled and kissed her daughter on the head, leaving the kitchen as soundlessly as Jyoti's ephemeral guilt.

SHEHZEEN

Shehzeen was sprawled out on the couch absentmindedly watching music videos while fully engrossed in a phone conversation with her friend Beth, who had been crying ever since she received new, credible information that her boyfriend actually *had* made out with Hillary in the mall's parking lot last week. As she was consoling her friend, Shehzeen's mother pushed open the front door with her foot and bustled in, trying her best to carry her briefcase, a garment bag, and a few items from the local gourmet grocery.

"How about a hand, Shezee!" she cried in frustration, almost stumbling in the doorway.

"Sorry, *Ammijaan!*" Shehzeen yelled, quickly jumping up from the couch. "I gotta call you back, Beth. Don't worry, he's not worth it anyway . . . I know, I know. Look, I'll call you, okay? Bye." She hung up and ran to her mom, who handed off the garment bag with a huff.

"Is it my dress?" Shehzeen asked excitedly, following her mom into the kitchen.

Her mother smiled, placing the groceries and her briefcase on the counter. "Go put it on. Let's see how the alterations came out." Unburdened by all the weight, Shehzeen's mom became as giddy as her daughter and skipped up the stairs with her to the girl's bedroom.

As her mother fell on the bed and kicked off her shoes, Shehzeen carefully unzipped and removed the bag, pulling out the dress. It was a lavender strapless formal with an embroidered top encrusted with crystals along the top border and a satin bottom that flowed like water. Though the women had seen it only two weeks ago when they chose it unanimously, they were again dazzled.

"Oh Shezee, it's so beautiful! It looks even prettier than in the store! Put it on!" her mom said, the British accent of her Indian convent-educated English becoming more pronounced with her excitement. Shehzeen quickly threw off her clothes and slipped into the dress while her mom made herself comfortable on the bed, rubbing her sore feet together.

"I loved that dress when I saw it because it reminded me of the ballroom gown I wore to my Go Away in college," her mother said.

Shehzeen was smoothing down the edges of her dress. "What's a Go Away, *Ammijaan?*"

"It's just like the prom, only in university. One last time to meet with your buds before you graduate."

"Who did you go with?" Shehzeen asked distractedly, scrutinizing herself in the mirror.

"Your *Abbajaan*, actually. We had just started dating. That was the first night we kissed too," she whispered shyly.

"Aw, really?" Shehzeen said, still looking at herself. "*Ammijaan*, doesn't this still look too loose on the waist and bust?"

Her mom got off the bed and stood behind her daughter to get a look. "Yes, it could be a little tighter. Do you want to go in tomorrow for another fitting?"

"But the prom's only a week away. Damn it! I can't believe they didn't get it right!" Shehzeen said, annoyed.

Her mother pinched the two seams in the back and pulled the dress tight. "Here, how does this look?"

Shehzeen looked up and down her dress. "Oh, *Ammijaan*, that's perfect. But are they going to be able to fix it in time?"

"See, this is why I tell you, you should learn a little sewing and cooking. It always comes in handy." She left the room and came back with a small sewing kit. As a child, despite having several servants, she had been taught to do many tasks thought necessary for any girl to know. At that time, wealth in India only truly spoiled sons, like Shehzeen's father. Her mother had grudgingly learned the tasks she considered menial, but was thankful for the lessons after immigrating to a place where the cost of labour was so high that her skills became immensely useful to a middle-class family. "Here, stand on your stool."

Shehzeen stood up on the stool as her mom began to pin the back of the dress. "So, *Ammijaan*, what did you and *Abbajaan* do at your prom?" she asked sheepishly.

"Oh, the same as every formal party," her mother replied from behind her daughter's back. "Ate dinner at a fancy hotel first and then went to the dance. We danced so much that night, I broke my heel! And your *Abbajaan* was so cute, he helped me to a table and put my foot in his lap while he tried to use his engineering skills to fix my shoe!" Mother and daughter laughed together. "It was then I said to myself, 'I think I'll marry this one.'"

"How did you tell your parents?" Shehzeen wondered. She had heard the perfect love story with a happy ending: though their love marriage was opposed by their conservative parents, they reluctantly acquiesced after the two told them that they were already living together in Hyderabad where they had both got jobs after college. Ironically, Shehzeen's grandparents' shared disappointment with their children for not marrying traditionally in an arranged marriage (nor, as they preferred, within the family) had brought the Muslim in-laws closer together during the planning stages of the wedding, and by the time of the *nikah*, both families had become very close.

"Oh boy! That was tough! Hold on," her mother said, stuffing a few pins into her mouth. She moved around on her knees to see the front of her daughter's dress and smoothed the satin folds of the skirt.

"It looks perfect, *Ammijaan!*" Shehzeen said, looking down at her mother. In her mid-forties, she still looked no older than twenty-five, and had a face so perfectly beautiful that she was more lovely with no makeup sitting on the couch than most of the delicately photographed models who graced the fashion magazines Shehzeen frequently read. The girl's heart filled with gratitude and respect for her mother, not only for her tailoring skills but also for her beauty, the undeniable source of her own door-opening physical attractiveness.

Her mother's mouth was still full, but she looked up at Shehzeen and smiled her love with her eyes while caressing the folds of the skirt. She stood up and dropped the pins back in her sewing kit. "It does look great! Take it off, and I'll redo the seams for you."

Shehzeen took off the dress carefully to avoid getting pricked by the pins, then sat next to her mother in her underwear as the latter searched for lavender thread.

"I tell you, I was a little scared to tell my parents," her mother said. "Actually, a lot! I was always afraid of disappointing them. But this time, I really feared them because not having an arranged marriage was considered *so* wrong. And it wasn't just worry about disappointing them!" she laughed.

"But I waited till I was home and brought in the whole family, because I knew my siblings and aunts and uncles would probably support me, and told them. They didn't blow up like I thought they would, but they were a lot more disappointed than I'd expected. It was really hard for me to see them like that. But I stuck to what I thought was right, and it was. Though they'll still not admit it!" They laughed together again.

When Shehzeen had been born, her mother realized that their generational gap would be at least as significant as hers and her parents', probably more given the new world in which her daughter would grow up. It was then that she promised herself she would never impose her views and values on her daughter and be open to her child's

Desilicious

reality and experiences. When Shehzeen came home with a boyfriend in seventh grade, she sat her down the next day and asked her several questions about why she wanted a boyfriend and what they would do together. Shehzeen had laughed and explained that dating didn't mean anything except going to the movies, dinners, and dances together (which was the truth, at the time), and her mother easily adjusted to this benign dating.

She assumed that Shehzeen's dates had remained as innocent since then, maybe some harmless kissing and petting with her more serious boyfriends. One day her husband mentioned that maybe she should talk to their daughter about sex after she had been dating Robert for over six months, so her mother sat Shehzeen down for another talk and tried to convey that she thought it best to wait till at least after college to engage in sex and only with boys she was seriously involved with. She told her daughter that she understood how the young girl's life was probably more different than she could understand, but one thing she was certain about was that no matter when Shehzeen had sex, she should always protect herself with a condom.

Bent closely over her daughter's gown, Shehzeen's mother remembered all the rumours that prom was the night many girls decided to lose their virginity. Before, when she'd heard the stories from other parents, she simply thought, *Oh, Shezee wouldn't do that*, but now, mindful of how ignorant her parents had been of the fact that she was living with her boyfriend, she said, "Shezee, I want you to know that I'm always going to be here for you to talk to, no matter what. I want you to always come to me and talk to me about anything you have questions about, okay?"

"Of course, *Ammijaan*, you're always the first person I go to, you know that," Shehzeen replied, sitting close to her mother for warmth.

"I know kids are having sex early these days, and maybe even a lot will be having sex on prom night. I know I've told you before and you're probably sick of hearing it, but I just want to say again that I personally think a girl is only mature enough to have sex once she's completed university." Shehzeen had heard her mother's advice a few times before and no longer squirmed at the topic. She had learned to simply let her mom talk and listen attentively, reassuring her mother that she understood.

"I know things are different in this country, and it may not be easy to live your life that way. But one thing I want you to remember, always, is that when you do start to have sex, no matter when it is, I want you to be sure to come to me with any questions. And always, *always* protect yourself."

"*Ammijaan*, I promise, whenever I have sex, I'll always be safe."

Unaware of the double meaning in her daughter's carefully prepared response, delivered with such precision that the "I'll always" could have easily been a slurred "I'm always," Shehzeen's mother gave her daughter a smile of relief and stroked her hair. Shehzeen leaned her head upon her mother's shoulder as she turned her attention back to her daughter's prom dress.

MEGHA

Megha sat at the breakfast table, feeling guilty as her mom juggled a pressure cooker, a rice cooker, and two uncovered pots, but not guilty enough to pull her exhausted body off the chair to help. Instead, she dropped her chin onto her hands that were palm-down on the table and kept watching her mom.

"Megha, I was talking to Mrs Richards, and she was telling me that her daughter bought a new dress for prom," her mother yelled to her in Hindi.

"Yeah, so?" Megha replied in English. Megha understood Hindi but had forgotten how to speak it, though her father constantly argued that she would easily pick it up if she just got the courage to try and practice. But between classes, her extracurricular activities, and studying French and Spanish, Megha didn't have the time to worry about practicing Hindi. Besides, her father, also a native of their hometown, usually spoke to her in his native English rather than semi-fluent Hindi, so she didn't think he really had a right to complain.

"Well, do you have a dress you can wear or do you need to buy a new one?" Megha would have liked to buy a new dress for prom; right now she was just planning on wearing the black dress she had bought for the wedding of her dad's colleague. But her parents had already paid sixty dollars for her prom ticket and even footed another fifty for the limo bill, since she was going stag at the time (Sooraj said he wanted to pay her back for that now that she was his date, but she'd refused and told him since she was wearing a dress she already owned and he had to rent a tux, it was an even trade).

"Oh, Ma, I forgot to tell you, you know that guy I told you about, Sooraj? He asked to be my date for prom last week, and I said yes. Is that okay?"

Megha's mom turned around, surprised. "The boy you like?"

"I never said I *like* like him, Ma. He's just a cool guy to hang around with."

"When did he ask you?"

"When did who ask what?" Megha's father asked, walking into the kitchen with a large black case that held his trombone, one of the several musical instruments he played and would use in his music classes at the local college.

"A friend of Megha's asked her to the prom," Megha's mom explained to her husband in Hindi.

"Uh oh, when?" he asked.

"At school last week. Me, Shezee, and Jyoti were all hanging out and their boyfriends and Sooraj came up. He was going stag with the guys and Jyoti started dropping all these hints so he was basically forced to ask me out."

"He's not your boyfriend or anything, is he? He just asked you to go as a friend, then?" Megha's mom asked in a serious tone.

"Yes, Ma," Megha replied, rolling her eyes. She continued to talk as if very tired or bored. "I don't have a boyfriend; I'm not dating anyone; I'm just going to the prom with some guy."

"Okay, okay, just asking, *beti*. Is it all right with you if your ma asks you about your life to make sure you're okay?" she asked rhetorically. "So, when is he picking you up?"

"Wait, wait, wait. You said *yes*?" her father asked, stunned.

"Well, I didn't want to make him feel bad, Dad! He's a nice guy; we're just going to prom together. We would've danced anyway, even if we went stag. And I don't want to be the third wheel when everyone else has a date. What's the big deal?"

Megha's father had always had crazy notions about dating, friendships, almost everything based on an extremist belief that all men were horrible beings. He constantly embarrassed her in front of her friends with crazy lectures (one was an apparently completely serious conversation about the evils of using pens or pencils because they were phallic symbols and how all her friends should type their papers rather than writing by hand) and sometimes just plain idiocy: doing bad impressions of Justin Timberlake singing or how "kids these days" dance.

Megha's friends found her father weird, but funny as well, though Megha always felt they were laughing at him not with him, especially since he seemed so serious when talking to them. More than embarrassed, she felt hurt that her friends would laugh at her father, but she didn't want to seem anal and scold them, so she took it out on her dad instead. Besides, she outright disagreed with a lot of what he said. Dating among teens, or as he called it, "psychologically manipulative raping," was one of his pet issues, so Megha knew she was about to get hell for going with Sooraj to prom.

"If it's no big deal, why must you go as a date?" he asked.

"It's just convenient! What did you want me to say? That I can't go with you because my dad thinks the prom is a patriarchal institution created to help boys deflower virgin girls in high school and then dump them later?" Megha was paraphrasing him from their argument about whether she should go to prom at all.

"Actually, yes. If you had some guts you could've said that," her father said, smiling. "But a simple, 'My parents don't let me go on dates; how about we just meet at the prom,' would've sufficed just as well."

"He was going stag with us anyway, Dad!" Megha implored. "We would've gone together, regardless." Her father always seemed to have an answer for everything and no matter how outlandish his responses initially seemed, there was something air-tight about them. Megha was already getting flustered with the expectation of ending up with nothing to say in response to him.

"All the less need to be his 'date.' I mean, doesn't that label just make you sick? You're *his* date. *His.* As if you're property." He turned around and started digging in the refrigerator.

"*Jaano*, I'm almost done with dinner. Wait, *na*," Megha's mother told him.

"Cool! You cooked? You get off early today or something?" Megha's mother was a computer programmer and when things at the office were slow, she would come home early to cook dinner, which was usually done by Megha's father between or after his classes.

"Dad, he's *my* date, too," Megha interrupted.

"Not the same. You know the double standard of sexuality. You're his pawn in this pathetically sexist institution, and you're just contributing to the establishment by going to this prom, and now with a date too!" Her father shook his head and gave her a disappointed look.

"Yeah, I *do* know about the double standard; you didn't care when *bhaiya* dated Komal in college. But with me, it's totally different, right?"

Her father chuckled. "Hold on, Megha," her mother said. "Trust me, you don't want to bring up your father's treatment of your *bhaiya* into this conversation, because it would just prove to you how truly crazy and consistent he is in what he believes. You have no idea the tough time he gave Gaurav."

Megha was quiet, intrigued at what her father must have said to her brother, remembering to ask him the next time he came home. "Well, you two dated."

"Correction, your mother dated," her father said.

"Megha, you know your father and I were in graduate school when we were seeing each other, and our parents had introduced us for the purpose of marriage. And I only had two or three boyfriends in India, where dating just means holding hands and *maybe* kissing. That was just a peck on the lips, not all dirty with tongues and groping like here."

Even as a young adult, Megha's mother never dreamt that she would have such conversations so casually with her daughter, especially with her husband present. Far worse were some of the topics her husband would talk to Megha and their older son about when they were in their early teens. She initially objected, but seeing how comfortable and familiar her children were with sex, she backed off and simply observed them with awed curiosity, her feelings of being an outsider, the only family member born and raised in India, resurfacing. But over the years, she had started to become more comfortable with the conversations herself and, like now, had even begun actively engaging in them.

Megha felt trapped without her mother's usual support, but she knew her mom was right. "Fine, whatever. The point is, can I go with him?"

"Well, you've already said yes. What's the point of asking us now?" her father said matter-of-factly. "And since *teri* Ma apparently thinks you're just going as friends with this guy and has given her okay, who am I to get in the way of your prom date, which statistics have proven lead to ninety percent of dumb girls giving it up to assholes who don't care two shits about them? Hey, you're a smart kid, I'm sure you're in that ten percent."

"Why do you talk like that with her?" Megha's mother said angrily. "Have some sense."

"Oh, come on, baby," he said, grinning. He turned to Megha. "You've heard people cuss before, haven't you, sweetie?"

"Yes, Dad," Megha said. "But it would be nice to have a father who wasn't as immature as a high school kid."

"What? Listen, I would've loved to have me as a dad. Come on, look at how hip I am." He started dancing in place while his wife laughed and his daughter couldn't help but giggle.

"Dad, please, you are so lame."

"Really?" he said with his hand covering his mouth in shock. "Oh no! I need to get a refund on that 'Hip Hip-Hop Dance Moves' tape I bought! Okay, so you're going to be a big ass sell-out, but here's the thing: you've *got* to bring the boy home a half hour before you leave so I can talk to him."

"Dad, no!" Megha cried. "Ma, you can't let him embarrass me. Dad, Sooraj is not like other guys, okay? He's smart. You can't embarrass me in front of him."

"Hmm," her father said. "Seems to me our little princess may have been slightly fibbing about just having platonic feelings for our Mr Sooraj."

Megha's mother smiled. "Well, she's got a little crush on him."

"Ma!" Megha yelled, feeling betrayed, knowing that her father would tease her mercilessly and make her feel even guiltier for saying yes to the date.

"Ah ha! Recipe for disaster, I tell you! That's it. Date's off!"

"Ma! Why did you have to open your mouth?" Megha said.

"Akash! I can't believe you sometimes. You have the sense of some street beggar," Megha's mother said.

"Okay, okay, fine. I was just kidding. God, it's not like she isn't talking to those friends of hers about this crap all the time. I can just tell that Shezee friend of hers has been around the block the way she's always trying to act like my *Dadi Ma* when I talk about anything sexual."

"Dad, you are so crude, I swear to God. Ma, this is why I don't want him talking to Sooraj," Megha reasoned.

"Don't worry, *beti*, I'll make sure he behaves," her mother said, patting her on the head.

"Well, one thing's for sure, your curfew is still ten," her father said, as he began to set the table for dinner.

"Ten! Dad, that's ridiculous! The parties don't even start till then!"

"You can come back, bring your little wuss friend you've got a crush on, and hang out here till eleven or later if your mom and I stay up, but you've got to be home by ten. Actually, ten-thirty, okay?"

"Dad, what's the point in even going to prom if I have to be back at ten!"

"Look, first I didn't want you going to prom, but we okayed it because you said you were going stag. Now you come home and tell us you're going with a guy, which you *know* I'm completely against. This is one thing you're gonna have to give to us now. There's no reason to stay out later than that on prom night or any night unless you're looking for trouble."

"Dad, this is crazy. I'm gonna look like such an idiot if I have to tell Sooraj I've gotta be back by ten-thirty! And he's such a decent guy; not *every* guy is an asshole like you're always trying to make out."

"Hmm, first question, why does *Chotki Rani* care so much about what Sooraj thinks? Second, all boys are assholes, some are just good at hiding it."

"Oh, I see! All guys are assholes. Okay then, Dad, what kind of guy *is* it okay to have sex with? How do you know if a guy's not an asshole? Or am I supposed to just never have sex? Never get married? Or here's a good one, are *you* an asshole?"

Megha's father smiled again at his daughter's strong rebuttal. "See, sweetie, that's the unfortunate dilemma of women in this age. The only man who's worthy of having sex with a woman is the guy who's just as hesitant, scared about getting her pregnant, worried about being called a slut, waiting for true love, marriage, 'the one,' just as much as the average girl today when she first has sex. He's the one to have, even before marriage if you want. That would be equal. Ten-thirty curfew, *chotki*."

Megha looked to her mother, who simply raised her hands in

surrender, and realized she'd have to give up. "God, Dad, you are so completely uncool!" she said.

"What? Look, I'm cool!" Megha's dad suddenly yelled, picking up a towel and throwing it over his head while punching the air. He started to rap, "Don't call it a comeback! I been here for years! Rockin' my peers, puttin' sucka's in fear! Makin' the tears rain down like a mon–soon! Listen to the bass go boom!"

Megha's mother laughed while their daughter shook her head. "God, Dad, you are such a dork!"

"What? That's L.L. Cool J, man! Primo old school stuff! You kids just don't know good music any more."

"Hey, but listen, Megha," her mother said, "you never told me what you're going to do about your prom dress. Just wear the old one you have then?"

"Yeah, it's the one I wore to Mr Beckett's wedding. It's nice enough."

"But it's not formal enough," her dad advised. "If you really wanna tear down the place, wear that new *lengha* we bought you. Now *that's* a prom dress. These crackers won't have nothing on that!"

Megha and her mom were silent, thinking. Megha finally spoke up. "Actually, that's not a bad idea."

No Gifts, Please

WANDERER

Kiran's almond-shaped eyes slowly adjusted to the darkness in the room. He is here, waiting. Her body language betrayed the true purpose of her being there with him, standing – almost touching but not quite, alone and somewhat vulnerable. Here at last – the two of them – the bride's sister and the groom-to-be, away from prying eyes of the pre-wedding party downstairs. What perverse twist of fate had led them to this rendezvous, this culmination of snatched glances and secret conversations? This was not to be an occasion for polite conversation. Would she allow herself to be taken, or in that moment of hesitation, in that vacuum between guilt and desire, would she be forced to take him?

She felt the tight embrace of Rohail's form against hers, his arms enveloping her shoulders and back, sliding snake-like up and down the length of her tissue silk *kameez* top. Her breathing tightened, and her eyes closed skywards as she felt the wet warmth of his lips, his curious tongue measuring the landscape of her tanned neck, carefully following her ornate silver chain. He pressed himself against her, pushing her, harder, back against the wall almost in harmony with the muffled *dhol* beats coming from downstairs. She could feel his hardening manhood as he ground his hips against her soft gyrating waist and push between her slowly spreading legs. His hands were now roaming her body freely, one massaging her silk-encased breast while the other probed inside her silk *salwar* around the back of her waist, making contact with the cleavage of her curvaceous rear.

The intoxicating intensity of the experience made her worry she would faint. Precariously perched on her narrow stiletto heels, sandwiched between the hard wall and Rohail's even harder torso. It was as if time stood still, no movement except a henna-laced hand clutching another, cleavage against chest rubbing in unison.

Oblivious to all surrounding senses, the pair, consumed by their arousal, were unaware of the cheerful chatter outside as the door handle slowly turned and a widening shaft of corridor light entered the darkened room. . . .

Desilicious

Love Poem

SMITA VIR TYAGI

firm walled chest
pressed into her back
face fanning her nape,
stray hair lightly rising
to the rhythm of breath.
solid,
gentle on her chest;
a length of leg curved beside hers

thigh to thigh, knee to knee
foot curled into smaller foot,
two "s"s snuggled into shape
deeply restful,
quiet, unmoving,
crisp, crimped sheet
telling the story of sleep.

The New Girl

ANITA AGRAWAL

She stood in front of the bathroom mirror topless and admired her newly developed breasts. She ran her hands around them, gently squeezing; eventually she held her palms over them and stood on her toes while she stuck out her chest, like a little robin, ready for flight. They looked a little awkward to her; she wasn't quite used to them yet. She hoped that the new bras her mom had bought for her would flatten the gigantic swellings, which had appeared over the course of the summer. A "B" cup! she thought. *Most girls aren't even wearing trainers yet!*

It was September, and school had just started. It was her final year of elementary, and Neha was already looking forward to the end. On the first day of class, she wanted to stay home and play sick. But she knew her mom was too intelligent for any of her tricks. At some point during the day her mom would realize what was bothering Neha, and they would have one of their long, tedious discussions about the facts of life. Neha didn't want to hear "the talk" again.

The talk was the one in which her mother would explain to her how women grew up and had to start behaving like young ladies, and most importantly, how they had to start being careful about boys. Neha had heard it again the past weekend, when they went shopping for bras. She had heard it when they went to India over the summer, where she was reminded to take proper precautions and try not to be alone with the "uncle-*ji*'s," and she had heard it when she started to menstruate last year. She never wanted to hear her mom talk about it again. Her mother's expression was permanently locked in Neha's memory as a cross between sympathy and disappointment. Disappointment that her baby girl had to grow up so soon.

Neha slipped her arms, one by one, into the straps of her new bra, and struggled to fasten the icy metal hooks. The straps weren't made of the soft familiar velcro she was used to. She looked at herself in the mirror again, and this time she was almost pleased with the way the intricate lace hugged the mounds. *Yes*, she thought, *this isn't so bad.*

Neha collected her school things and hurried to put them into her knapsack, which she kept tucked under her bed. A look of embarrassment crossed her face when she picked it up and her drawing pad fell out, opening to the picture that she had drawn the night before. Her heart raced.

What would her mother say if she saw this? Neha envisioned it now – rage and anger would hide her mother's confusion and disappointment. Disappointment – that her daughter had turned into a typical *Canadian* girl. At first she didn't understand what her mother meant by this. But over time she had come to realize that it was something her mother referred to as negative. To her mother, a *Canadian* girl was someone who was interested in boys, collected posters from teen magazines, went out on dates, and played spin-the-bottle at basement parties with her friends. Of course, Neha was not such a girl.

She imagined what her own response to her mother would be. Would she fumble for words to explain to her mother that sometimes she thought about these things, that sometimes she dreamed of standing naked and being held and caressed by pairs of random hands? These thoughts alone made her body tingle all over. She dreamed of hands running across her body, touching her breasts and between her legs, but to her mother she would try to explain that these were just cartoonish drawings and meant nothing. Would her mother understand? Would she trust Neha? Neha, who now had womanly breasts? Neha, who played soccer everyday after school with boys? Would her mother know? She tore up the drawing – *crrrshhh, crsshh, crssssh* – into tiny pieces, and disposed of it – like always.

~

There weren't many new faces in class that year. Neha noticed one in particular, however: Cheryl. They began to hang out together at recess, to everyone's displeasure. The other girls in the class warned Neha that Cheryl wasn't a good girl, that she was Jay's ex-girlfriend.

Neha ignored what the other girls said because she liked Cheryl.

She didn't look like an average eleven-year-old; she somehow seemed older than the rest of them, womanly, if that were possible.

Today, Cheryl was wearing tight elastic jeans; Neha had asked for jeans like that a few weeks earlier at the mall, ones that would make her look slimmer and taller, but her mother objected. Neha looked down at her own yellow stirrup pants. There was a hole in one of the knees, from the gym class when David had body-checked her during soccer. She knew her mother would make her dispose of them as soon as she saw the tear. She was glad she could wear them until then.

It was October, and an early winter was setting in. It would be hard to spend the last few recesses outside without a sweater. Cheryl didn't mind the cold weather; she usually spent her recesses outside, regardless. This recess she wore Jay's jacket – they had started going out again. The sleeves on his jacket were too long on Cheryl's thin frame.

Neha and Cheryl headed out over the fence and out of the schoolyard. Cheryl lit a cigarette, and they found a comfortable place to sit on the grass. Cheryl began to recount her weekend. "I went over to Mike's house this weekend with Jay and Bill," she said.

"Who are Mike and Bill?" Neha asked.

"They're from Simon Fraser."

"Really?" Neha inquired. "What grade?"

Cheryl sensed Neha's excitement, but it didn't faze her. "Nine and ten," she said. "Man, Jay and I got completely loaded at his place. Mike's dad has everything – vodka, gin, rum, and beer. My stepdad's bar isn't as big."

"I see," Neha said. She had never had such an experience.

"Yeah, it kinda sucked 'cause we played strip poker and me and Jay lost big time. I've never lost all my clothes before, but Jay – he was pissed. He was down to his underwear. He gets embarrassed in front of those guys I guess, being as short as he is."

"Did you get in trouble when you got home?"

"My stepdad wasn't too thrilled that I came home so late. I got in at about two in the morning. Those jokers, they wouldn't let us go – they wanted to take pictures of me and Jay naked together, they said since we didn't have any money to give them that we had to, because it would only be fair. They wouldn't stop teasing us on how they would tell the whole school about how Jay lost, if we didn't do what they said. Jay was really angry. So Mike said he would settle on a kiss and a pic of me alone. At that point Jay just wanted to leave. He even cussed at Mike for taking the pic. I don't know why, it's not like they hurt me or him or anything like that. Anyways, so we left, and then we made out under the stairs of my porch, until my stepdad caught us. Jay's such a better kisser than Mike, anyways."

Neha tried to hide her shock and surprise at everything Cheryl told her. Moreover, she hoped her pity wouldn't show, as she had begun to feel sorry for Cheryl, whom all the girls in class disliked, and whom boys often teased. Her parents had divorced too, and her stepfather sometimes hit her with a belt after he drank.

At the same time, Neha was filled with a remote sense of self-satisfaction that she had two loving parents, was popular in school, got good marks, and never had to worry about anyone taking pictures of her naked. Until that moment, she thought that Cheryl had everything Neha always wanted: she was slim, tall, pretty, had nice red hair, and got lots of attention from guys who wanted to go out with her, something Neha only got for having large breasts.

Neha looked at the cloud of cigarette smoke surrounding Cheryl's small head. She looked so collected, so calm, her serenity put Neha to shame. "Want a toke?" Cheryl asked. Neha wasn't exactly sure what a toke was, but she knew what Cheryl meant. "No, thanks. I don't smoke," Neha said with a poised confidence that only she knew was meant to cover her confusion.

~

It was six PM and Neha sat against the door of her room, crouched on her toes in case anyone came in. She started drawing the same picture again. A picture of her naked body, held by hands – touching every part of her. It excited her, and she drew feverishly both with excitement and fear of being caught. Hands over her breasts, between her legs; touching her, feeling her, rubbing her breasts like she sometimes did to herself while standing in front of the mirror. She wondered what it would be like if it actually happened.

"Neha!" her mother called. "Come and eat dinner."

She quickly tore up her drawing, but suddenly felt the kind of nausea she'd had when she was younger and her friend Shauna had showed her the tattered pictures of naked grown-ups she had found in the alley. In one of the pictures, between the water stains, Neha could see the brightly coloured pink flesh between a woman's thighs, spread wide. The woman was smiling, though the flesh between her legs looked like it was alive and throbbing, like it would burst forth at any moment and spew out blood. In some of the other pictures the men looked like they were attacking the women. At the time she wanted to slug stupid, idiotic Shauna for showing the pictures to her, but instead she ran to the school washroom to be sick, even though nothing came out. Unlike her own drawings, such images scared her: images of people that Neha didn't know, and that Neha believed could not feel. Women she wished to be like at times, hands caressing them – but women who wore the same stoic expression Cheryl did while telling her story about Mike, Bill, and Jay.

Suddenly, Cheryl's hardened face flashed before her. Her chapped pink skin, bright copper hair, thin slender nose with a bulbous tip, and beady black eyes – eyes that looked like thin, black, almond-shaped slits. Maybe Cheryl was a woman like the women in the pictures, a woman who had forgotten how to feel.

Neha dragged herself into the dining room. Her mother placed a plate in front of her. "Neha, *beta*, eat your dinner," her mother said in Hindi. She paused and looked Neha over. "Neha, don't wear that shirt anymore, *beta*, it's too tight on you now. You don't want to start looking like a big girl already, do you? We'll go shopping this weekend and buy you some new clothes. Eat your dinner and make sure you change before Papa gets home."

Colombo to Haputale

ANNIE DIJKSTRA

I started feeling the climate change, the freshness that I had missed for so long on the coast. Lying with my head on the pillow, I could see the tops of the coconut palms alternating with straighter trees. Creaking softly through the paddy fields with the moon jumping over the paths, the train bounced roundly as we creaked higher and higher.

The train took a long, slow journey that moved from the humid coast through spring woods to frosty moor-like spaces and wilder hills before stopping in the stepped tea plantation area. I would relish sleeping without a fan for the weekend. The train made two journeys a day through stations that had not changed their procedures for fifty years. The stationmaster still held aloft the leather hoop to be collected by each driver to ensure that the single track was never over-occupied. Drivers still cited "elephant halt" on their trip logs at the ultimate in natural necessity – waiting patiently for the elephant to pass – or using it as an excuse to deliver food from the humid plains to a relative living close to the tracks. I had chosen the night train this time, along with families carrying enough lunch packets to last a week. During the trip, I could relish hanging from the duckboards as we rounded steep terrifying curves, daring myself to lean more, watching the coast recede and the mists rise, but most of all, I wanted to watch the vegetation change from broad leaves to refined, smaller and crazier ones as we rose higher and higher.

I had taken this trip before, but in broad daylight. This time I purposely chose the night train and a two-berth carriage. We sat opposite each other recovering from the scrabble of boarding. Smiling with glee at having escaped, enjoying the privacy. Holding hands without being pushed or gawked at. One large white girl and one small brown one.

I felt your distance that night for too long. Craving for us to be lying in the bed together. Wetness surprising me against the plastic seat as I watched your hand pushing the bag onto the luggage rack. I yearned for the creases in your jeans. I wanted you. Your silver rings caught the light from the suburban stations as you explained your difficult day enduring a computer crisis and a man who had crept into your garden to steal clothes from the line. The power cuts in Colombo had enabled emboldened men to jump walls and servers were in crisis all over town. People sweated as the cuts grew to eight-hour stretches with nothing to do but sleep and shower and talk.

As the moon lifted she calmly and silently preoccupied my mind and vision. If we hit a straight stretch for long enough I could study the ridges and bumps carefully. Reassuringly, her consistent presence lured me. I hung between sleep and wakefulness, the rhythm not strong enough to perk me up, but not soft enough to lull me.

The round edges of the bunks eased into the harsh metal posts with a crisp sheet lying roughly around them. As we started kissing I watched the last of the buffalos I was to see for a while, moonlight shadowing their angular hips. The train climbed higher and I pushed my tongue into the space between your teeth and lips, running it back and forth, enjoying remembering how they felt, where the ridges and gaps were. Reunited. I began to visit favourite body parts and felt your nipples stiffen against your shirt, taking tours to curves and arches and checking that all was in order. You leaned against the carriage door, making sure that a stray ticket inspector, an over-excited teenage boy, or a sleepy child did not stumble upon us.

The train would arrive at stations in a roar of steam, noise erupting, people lumbering into arms of families, dinners being bought, and shouts of greetings and farewells.

Your darkness was hidden in the dim carriage. Frustrated, I moved to see you properly. You were so quiet I was surprised where you next surfaced on my body, touching me with a body part that immediately awoke to its own arousal. I could see you in the half-darkness, the light glancing over your strong shoulders reflecting the firmness of upper arms as you moved over me. Sometimes I would lose sight of you completely and then suddenly the moon would show me the line of your cheek, the strength of your shoulder, and occasionally your eyes, looking intently at your favourite parts of me. I shone in comparison, getting brighter as it got darker. I caught sight of your back, muscles imitating potential pleasure, moving carefully in the mirror above the tiny carriage sink as the train arrived at station after station, the flickering helping me to concentrate on predicting your next move.

Hair tickled my thighs and back and prickled my cheeks as you kissed my neck. I impatiently fucked your mouth with my fingers. The softness of your tongue against my rough forefinger. Pressing more fingers into you, your greed making me impatient. I slipped my hands between your thighs, you moving away angrily, but I was able to glide my fingers far enough to feel the gap and the smoothness leading down there. I salivated as I felt how easily I could slide my hand away.

I could hear other passengers clumsily pressing against the carriage door, in contrast to your masterful tracing of the boundaries of my pleasure. So studiously you charted the fathoms, knowing so much more about the terrain than I had even realized existed. Impatiently I would demand and cajole, but resisting all campaigns you marched away from easy victory. Exploring new territories to conquer, I would lose a sensation abruptly and gain a continent without knowing it even existed. Then bringing me to view valleys as far as the eye could see you would pull me back from the edge in haste, to base camp, to rethink. Rude circuit breakers switched on. You easily pulled away and laughed as I roared with impatience, calling it my western greediness. You'd rather linger for the added benefits.

You continued to write this new story, at times a Shakespearean tragedy with curtain drops that rudely suspended the drama. Scenes moved forward as I anxiously looked forward to the ending. The twists and turns of heaven and hell – I breathed slowly, careful not to expire in bliss.

Against a backdrop of Horton plains and heather, craggy barren branches were illuminated by the moon as I dropped my head backwards to watch the world upside down. Bats hovered over the moors. I lost sense of where I was, images of a life before flashing rapidly through my mind. Feeling your slender strength pressed against the foot of the bed, slight movements of the train rippled through your legs, making you press more heavily into me, your chin nudging gently as if to usurp the tongue's kingly position. Your tongue soothed areas where your fingers had been. Sometimes I did not know if you were touching me or not, as lost as I was in air and mouth on me.

And when held suspended in a vacuum, I felt a momentary escape from the surrounding bliss; with the clarity of an owl's eye I saw how life was so different before. Flat, I was suspended somehow in a buffer zone of calm joy circled by the rage outside. The train traversed through more challenging terrain, switching back and forth, as we finished the last push to the hills.

The smell of dew on tea arose towards Nuwera Eliya, pickers chatting on the way to work as we ambled past. I gasped as you entered me, finally using the energy of the train and my gradual letting go to work yourself further and further into me. Your fingers moved with the train and me, persistent and fair. I lost sense of time and place and motion. Dropping into the valley as we climbed upwards, I greedily pushed and pulled. My edges replete bursting from within myself sated. Your first gasps rose slightly over the noise of the tracks. I felt your hunger now as patiently as you had observed mine. The closeness of coming that you were now allowing me gently and kindly and cruelly and gave to me like a prize, angrily I grasped it, quickly craving self-sufficiency again. I lost myself and suddenly found a new me I had forgotten about.

I began to think again. Returned to a world of arrivals, timetables, discomfort, and the din of the train and other passengers. The berth looked bare as sunlight leaked in through the slimy glass.

Haputale, a sickly village clinging to the mountain edge, swung into view, and I sat up, the bleak light revealing the tacky hoardings for "Valley View" and "Happy Traveller" guesthouses. The touts rushed to meet the train. Grabbing my toothbrush and book and my bag from the luggage rack, quickly finding that extra jumper, I rush out of my messed-up berth to reach the guesthouse before they reach me. I am hungry for a string hopper breakfast.

Snake Poem

SALACIOUS SISTER

Her room is a womb-like cave
rust-coloured, filled with knick-knacks and magic.
Colourful goddess images on the wall
Inspire her to delve and deepen.

She is teaching herself to come
on her thick, red futon.
Touching to recapture a gift that was stolen,
temporarily removed,
orgasm-napped.

High on grace and grass she sets the stage
silk nightie, coconut oil, and candles.
Perfume.

She wears panties because
she is afraid to see all of herself at once,
and frightened of the faces of imagined men,
who might be watching,
as with cold fingers she skips down her belly.

Comes up with a thousand fears,
but continues
(stopping only to jot down a poem).

The girl has a tattoo on her sternum and right breast.
A small snake –
purple on one half of its wriggly body
green on the other.

Colours of passion, embedded in her skin at eighteen.

She circles the snake with coconut oil.

At twenty-three she begins
to understand its significance.

Jasmine Rain

R. ISMAIL

It was Thursday
When I came to
It started when
You pulled the jasmine out of my hair
And whispered in my ear
With that Dravidian tongue
That I couldn't let you stop
You would go on and on
Till I felt the rain
And you started
Fingers burned inside me
Sambar and *idli*
For lunch
You rubbed away my *pottu*
Said it was too
Distracting
I curled my toes
To hide the
Metti
And you spread my legs
A little wider
Two fingers now
Inside of me
And the burning was starting to
Feel too good
I whispered for you to stop
And then
Your tongue was there
I called on

Parvati
And Saraswati
But it was Kali
Who responded
She told me
To sit still
That I would be a woman
Soon
And that it
Would feel too good
To turn back
So I didn't.

Journey

NAVJIT SINGH

5:30 AM

"Hemant, wake up! If we don't catch the train in time our whole day will go wasted, and you know your *Bua* has come all the way from London. She's never going to forgive us if we don't make it to Agra this time around."

The sharp tone broke my routine. No self-respecting, spoiled Indian male would like to be in his mother's bad books – including myself. So I unhinged myself out of the bed, threw off the blanket, and headed for the bathroom to get ready.

"Oye, *nephewji*, can't you even greet your aunt, eh?" Rani *Bua* called out as she saw me enter the bathroom.

"Surely you don't want to smell my bad breath," I smiled back.

"Okay, love, forgiven this time around, *par agli baar*, you'll have to kiss me on the cheek!" she chuckled.

5:55 AM

Breakfast was a quick affair as we had to catch the 6:30 AM Taj Express from the New Delhi railway station. I had just enough time to haul the food basket stuffed with *paranthas*, *achaar*, and dry *matar paneer sabzi*, and then trot behind mother and *Bua*, who were heading towards the three-wheeler stand.

The morning was fresh and the air crisp, the rose tint still streaking the clouds. Elderly folk were streaming back from the park after their morning *bhajans*. My mother greeted a few of her friends from afar as we continued towards the stand.

"*Behanji, itni subah*, where do you want to go?" the rickshaw *wallah* asked.

"Station, *bhai*, and better hurry up," Mother said.

"*Behanji*, thirty rupees." Mother balked at the price, so the three of us unseated ourselves from the three-wheeler we had taken control of.

The other driver was more considerate. A brown, wizened face, creases running across his forehead, a *bidi* just about sticking out of his *paan*-stained lips. Must have been forty years old, but the burden of living had added another ten years or so to his face.

"*Behanji*, twenty-five rupees and I'll take you straight to the station."

"*Mamaji*, it's getting late. Let's just take this auto," I prodded my mother, who acquiesced quickly lest she upset *Bua's* trip so early on.

6:00 AM

Off we scooted, across the Medical Institute, where rows of people were still asleep on the footpath, and over the Safdarjung fly-over, which arches over Delhi's first airport. We rode past the wide leafy roads of Lutyen's New Delhi, where sprawling bungalows are set in yawning lawns for the ruling elite to recline in the faith of their own abilities.

6:20 AM

Finally, we sputtered into the New Delhi railway station. Even at this early hour one could detect signs of the oncoming storm of travellers, as vendors prepared tea and fried samosas in several days' old oil, beggars with distorted limbs writhed across the platforms to "cash generating" points near the air-conditioned coaches, and the red-shirted coolies made a beeline for our baggage.

"No *yaar*, no help required. *Arre nahin re, nahin ji, bilkul nahin,* leave it please!" I spoke quickly to dissuade the coolies before they could pounce on our sole and precious food basket.

We knew the Taj Express would depart from Platform 5 and it was already waiting. Clutching out tickets, we ran across the overhead bridge to make way to our coach, A5, seats number 34, 35, and 36.

6:25 AM

As Mother and *Bua* sat comfortably cross-legged on the seats, I placed our precious basket on the overhead rack.

"I'll get the water," I volunteered and ran quickly to fetch two Bisleri bottles. "No *yaar*, not the cold ones, just normal ones," I said irritably as I checked the time.

6:27 AM

Once inside again, I closed my eyes since I didn't want to witness the grime and din outside our coach windows. Mother and *Bua* had started to catch up on family gossip.

6:29 AM

"*De de pyar de, pyar de, pya de, de de pyar de,*" sang a hoarse voice from the other end of the compartment.

There appeared Saira Bano (as we came to know her name later), her hair oiled back into a single braid, forehead streaked with blood-red *sindoor*, kohl-lined, yes, garish pink lipstick, a dozen blue and green bangles on each arm, and wearing a matching pale blue *salwar kameez* suit.

Her wrists clapped rhythmically as she progressed down the compartment, and flirted with a young couple who were making their first trip to see the Taj.

"*Arre* congratulations, my dear Majnu, your wife looks just like his Laila. Shall I sing for you? Just might ease the journey, *haan!*"

The irritated husband snapped, "Just move off now, leave us alone. Isn't there anyone else you can pester?"

That's when Bano Sahiba saw us non-honeymooners and scurried over. She clapped her hands, looked straight at my mother, and cried "*Memsahib*, my name is Sairo Bano. Can I sing for you? May your children live for 100 years, and may they beget lots of children."

"Sure," my mother responded wearily.

At this open invitation Bano Sahiba straightened herself, focussed

~ *157*

her eyes intently somewhere outside the window and, just as she opened her mouth, the train lurched forward. But the unexpected motion didn't ruffle her, and in her hoarse voice she began to sing.

"*Ai malik tere bande hum. . . .*" It was an appropriate piece for the morning, but she quickly followed it up with, "*Kajra muhabat wala, akhiyon mein aisa dala. . . .*"

Mother quickly opened her purse, and handed fifty rupees to her.

"*Sau sau saal jiyo Bibiji*, bless your husband and sons, may they live for along time and take care of you."

"Well, that's my nephew, bless him," smirked *Bua*.

Time stood still as she took my head in her hands to bless me. My eyes, which had been admiring Bano Sahiba's slender waist, now refused to look into hers. Me, foreign educated and returned, an inheritor of the New India, being blessed by . . . her?

But Bano Jaan was too quick. As she uncupped her hands from my head after blessing me, she winked at me slyly. That's when I saw the tattoo on her arm and cringed inside as I recalled:

Condom: Rs. 5

Rickshaw to the Defense Colony Bridge: Rs. 15

Blowjob: Rs. 20

The fear of almost being caught with him: Priceless.

Mrs Gupta Visits the Gynecologist

REENA SHARMA

"Oh Mummy, I know you've never been to this kind of doctor, but . . ." Amit paused, running his fingers through his hair. "It's very important . . . you know, to catch diseases . . . and such-nots . . . down *there*," he said, finishing in a half-whisper.

Mrs Gupta sat in the living room chair, examining her stitching, her bifocals balanced on the bridge of her nose. She was trying to stitch a Krishna pillow for the living room. Krishna's flute was slightly crooked. She unraveled the stitch, then looked up at her son and nodded. He shuffled his feet in discomfort, avoiding his mother's eyes. She did not understand why she had to go to this kind of doctor for such an examination. It was really quite embarrassing and improper. Why, she was an old woman! What business was it of anybody's to know what was down *there*?

But ever since she had come to live with her son, he had become obsessive about her health, monitoring her blood pressure and sugar level, making her cut down on sweets and fried foods. So much fuss and for what? Everyone would die some day, she reasoned.

"Who knows, maybe you have cancer . . . not that I expect them to find cancer, mind you, but better to find it early than to have regrets." Amit glanced at his wife Sarita, who was sitting at the dining room table paying bills. She seemed oblivious to their conversation, but secretly found it amusing and rather cute the way Amit fretted about his mother.

"Sarita, why don't you fill Mummy in on the details about her . . . uh . . . Pap smear? I'm running late," he said in a muffled voice. And although Amit was not late for anything, he pretended to look at his watch, then rushed out of the house, red-faced and coatless.

Neither woman spoke for a full five minutes.

"Would you like a cup of tea, *Mata?*" Sarita asked, getting up from the table.

Mrs Gupta nodded.

Sarita patted her on the arm as she passed by. "Don't let Amit make you nervous. You know how he is. Always worrying about small things. Everything will be fine tomorrow."

But that evening, after her rose-scented bath and prayers, Mrs Gupta hardly slept. Her head swam with questions and doubts. What if her doctor was a man? She looked up at the portrait of Vinod, her late husband, hanging on the bedroom wall. A garland of dried marigolds circled the frame. He was the only man who had ever touched her down *there*. Even when she was pregnant with Amit, the village midwives had taken care of everything.

What would it be like to visit this doctor who looked at a woman's private parts? Such a shameful job! Would he have to get on his knees and peer up? Or would he lie on the floor while she squatted on top of him, much like the way a mechanic did to a car when he looked for oil leaks? Or maybe there would be a special machine. Oh yes! America had so many wonderful gadgets. Maybe he wouldn't have to look up *there* at all. Maybe the hospital had a machine that would know just what was up *there* without having to actually go up *there*. It would be like one of those metal detectors at the airport that one put their bags through. It would beep if something were wrong. A small, harmless beep that didn't scare anyone.

Mrs Gupta grappled with her anxiety until two in the morning. When she finally fell asleep, she had the same recurring dream she had been having for many months now. She was standing on the edge of a cliff looking down into the foaming, wind-swept ocean. The waves churned like boiling tea water, crashing against the boulders, lapping onto the shore, before slipping back into the sea. But Mrs Gupta could not look away. Her eyes were fixed on Vinod. He swam back and forth, his strong, brown arms cutting the water like an ocean god. He would look up at her, smile, his hair glistening with the water's light, and beckon her in. Her body would grow tense and quivery. Vinod seemed so far away and so close in the same moment. She felt a shiver run through her, felt the longing in her feet to jump, to leave the earth and lose herself in liquid and light. Then, gasping, she would awaken, the sound of the ocean roaring in her ears. She was always too afraid to jump.

In the morning, Mrs Gupta decided to wear her prettiest white underwear, the ones with the lace trim that Sarita had given her for her fifty-sixth birthday. Since her husband's death, she wore only white. She sprinkled baby powder between her legs to sweeten her smell. She even did a few yoga postures in case the doctor asked her to get into an uncompromising position. "Better prepare for the worst," she thought aloud as she posed like a palm tree, bending into the wind.

Mrs Gupta was very careful when she sat in the passenger's seat of Sarita's car, keeping her legs slightly open so as not to trap any moisture down there. The smell of baby powder rose in the air and overpowered the scent of Sarita's pine-scented air freshener. Sarita could tell her mother-in-law was nervous by the way she fidgeted with her fingers. They hardly talked during the trip to the clinic, except to discuss the weather and the Dollarama sale at Kmart that coming weekend.

At the clinic, Sarita signed in for Mrs Gupta and took a seat next to her. Mrs Gupta was watching the TV screen. A skinny, toothless woman on Jerry Springer threw a chair at another guest who had very messy hair and wore no shoes. The skinny woman screamed insults, but all Mrs Gupta could hear was the crowd's laughter and the bleep-bleep-bleep of the censors. Her eyes drifted away from the television and to the other patients. An elderly woman with puffy white hair and a blue cardigan sat across from her reading a copy of *Better Homes and Gardens*. Mrs Gupta wondered if she were here for the same purpose. She wanted to ask her what colour her underwear was and whether she had scented herself with powder, or perhaps she had come without it.

After fifteen minutes of musing about the other patients' hygienic rituals, she heard her name called: "Mrs Goop-tah." A young, curly-haired girl with dimples was waiting by the door that led inside. Mrs Gupta quickly shuffled to her feet, the folds of her sari falling around her ankles. She picked up her black handbag, looked back at Sarita who nodded with assurance, and followed the girl inside.

"Can you please stand on the scale?" the dimpled girl asked.

Mrs Gupta did as she was asked.

The girl shifted the weights around.

"One hundred and forty-five pounds," she said brightly and wrote

Reena Sharma

it down on her chart. Next she proceeded to take Mrs Gupta's blood pressure and asked her a few personal questions. Mrs Gupta did her best to answer them without blushing.

Ten minutes later, she sat in a tiny room wearing a paper robe, shivering. Her underwear, bra, petticoat, blouse, and sari lay neatly folded on a nearby chair. Her shoes were tucked underneath. She could not believe they made her take *all* of her clothes off. The papery robe crunched with her every movement and exposed most of her back. Mrs Gupta felt uncomfortable not being properly dressed. How could one be dignified in such attire? She thought about the women on Jerry Springer who lifted their blouses to flaunt their breasts at the audience. She tried to pull the robe more tightly around her waist, but only succeeded in tearing it, exposing her left buttock.

In a few minutes, a woman with blonde hair and crinkly eyes walked in.

"Hello," she introduced herself. "I'm Dr Hester. And you must be. . . ." She glanced down at the chart she was carrying. "Mrs Goop-tah?"

Mrs Gupta nodded, shifted nervously, and wondered why Americans always said her name like it was two words instead of one. Goop and Tah. She wanted to shake Dr Hester's hand, but was afraid that one more false move and the rest of her paper gown would unravel around her, like one of her stitchings.

"Now, Mrs Goop-tah, can you lie down for me?" Dr Hester asked in a pleasant voice. Mrs Gupta nodded, smiled, and laid down.

"You are from India?"

"Yes, yes," Mrs Gupta smiled. "I live with my son and his wife and one child named Raju. He is seven . . . no, eight . . . a very good boy," she gushed with pride.

"That's lovely." The doctor placed her stethoscope on Mrs Gupta's chest.

"Now breathe in deeply."

Mrs Gupta inhaled and exhaled as the doctor shifted the stethoscope from one part of her chest to another.

"I've always wanted to go to India," Dr Hester continued. "To see the temples and elephants . . . and of course, the people."

Mrs Gupta began to feel a little more at ease. First, because the doctor was a woman, and second, because Dr Hester wanted to know about India. She liked the way the doctor's glasses hung on a gold

Desilicious

chain around her neck and the way her lips shone with a tint of pink gloss. Her voice was soothing, with a lilt, and her breath smelled like cinnamon gum.

"Now I'm going to check your breasts for any lumps," the doctor informed her. "Please lift your arms up." Mrs Gupta did as she was asked.

The doctor's hands were warm. She squeezed and pressed around the older woman's breasts, feeling between the pockets of fatty tissue. Mrs Gupta liked how the warmth of the doctor's fingers spread throughout her entire body, like a towel just removed from the dryer and held close to one's body. She could feel her body loosen, surrender, and give in to the hand that was soothing her muscles, speaking to her bones and flesh.

"You should also make an appointment for a mammogram if you haven't had one," Dr Hester said. "Just tell the nurse at the front desk." Then she put on her glasses and wrote something in the chart.

Mrs Gupta nodded and tried to remember the last time someone had touched her breasts. It seemed so long ago when she and Amit's father had been together. The last two years of his life he was sick, and hardly touched her at all. She had spent most of that time taking care of him, feeding and bathing him, reading aloud passages from the *Bhagavad Gita*. She tried to reach into her memory for a time even before that, when being with her husband was not contingent upon good health or whether the clothes were ironed, or the dishes dried and put away. But she could not reach that far back.

Dr Hester moved towards Mrs Gupta's bottom half.

"Mrs Goop-tah, can you move down a little?" she asked in a sing-song voice.

Mrs Gupta jiggled her hips.

"More . . . more . . . a little more, that's fine." She stopped jiggling.

"I'm going to need you to put your legs in these metal stirrups," she requested.

Dr Hester took her feet and gently glided them into the stirrups. It was cold, but Mrs Gupta was beginning to enjoy these new sensations. She especially liked how the doctor told her what she was going to do, as if she were asking permission to touch her.

At first Mrs Gupta was embarrassed about having someone so close to her private areas, but as she began to let go of her shame and rigidity, she did not mind this closeness. She felt rather grand, like a queen, her body revered, held up by two metal stirrups, wide open. It was like giving birth, only without the pain or the child.

Mrs Gupta could not see what Dr Hester was doing down there. But she knew that her body trusted the doctor. She felt something wet glide inside of her, probing its way into her darkest being. She lay still and let the doctor wiggle the instrument inside of her.

"Very good," Dr Hester said after a minute or so.

"Now I'm going to feel your uterus."

Mrs Gupta felt a stirring inside of her. At first, it was a slight tickling sensation. But slowly it spread across her belly like the slow, rhythmic travel of an ocean wave. She sensed the soft unfolding and opening of her flesh. She felt a vibration inside of her, a deepening response much like the hum that one felt when chanting a mantra. It seemed to almost lift her, this sacred force greater than Dr Hester's gloved fingers, that traveled to that part of her body that lay dormant all these years, locked and stored like a secret treasure buried in the ocean's floor. And now someone had finally come to open it, to clear away the algae and fish droppings, to say this is who you are, and have always been.

How come Amit's father had never made her feel this way, she wondered, never made her body sing like this, yearning to be opened and held and loved without expecting anything in return?

Or maybe he had.

And her mind reached back, back to where it could not go earlier. And she saw Vinod, his arms circling her waist, and she pushing him away, running to the kitchen to check on the rice pudding. And again, when he had written her a poem in Hindi in the early years of their marriage, left it next to her pillow as she slept, and how she had never told him how beautiful it was, and he had never asked. And when Amit was born, she spent more time nurturing her son than her husband because a child was so easy to love. Giving love was easy for mothers, but why was it so difficult to ask for love, to accept love and all the pleasures it entailed?

When Dr Hester left, Mrs Gupta slowly dressed herself. Her body felt different: light, tingly, grounded. She wished there was a full-length mirror in the room, so she could see herself, really see herself from head to toe. She took a deep breath and felt the air enter her lungs, filling her belly, expanding her heart. And then she exhaled. She felt as if she had been living in a darkened room all these years, and now someone had opened a window, pulled back the curtains, and allowed the light to enter. And here it was, spreading through her body, this warm radiance that came with the knowledge that her body was not just an abode for her soul, like many of the holy books had insisted. But rather, her body *was* her.

In the lobby, Sarita noticed that her mother-in-law had a tiny smile on her lips. Her face looked less strained, relaxed.

"How did it go?" she asked.

"Fine, fine," Mrs Gupta replied, not wanting to divulge any details.

"I'm supposed to come back for a mammogram," she informed Sarita.

"Ooh, I've heard they can be painful," Sarita murmured, cringing. She made her way to the front desk to set up an appointment, wondering how Amit would explain mammograms to his mother.

That evening Mrs Gupta dreamed of her husband again. He was still in the ocean, frolicking in the waves, smiling, beckoning her in. But this time she was not afraid. She closed her eyes and plunged into the blue waves.

Debashish does Delhi

IGNATIUS J.

STORY THE FIRST

When Debashish walked down a street, anyone walking towards him would pass by without noticing him. If it were a desi walking towards him, he or she would usually turn the other cheek in the fine Gandhian tradition of all desis who didn't want to recognize poor, ugly, fat, bald, or otherwise unpalatable desis as having any link to their species. However, Debashish wasn't poor, ugly, fat, or bald. He was the "other," the otherwise unpalatable. Specifically, he walked, talked, and generally lived in airs of insignificance. He was minute, miniscule.

It was therefore no surprise that on his first visit to India he was pleasantly surprised when people looked up to him as a *pardesi*. This more than anything else gave him the confidence to talk to Amrita that day. He had come to India with his parents after insisting that if he was to marry it must be with a true and pure Indian girl. His parents had entertained the notion that as they were now Canadians, he ought to marry a Canadian girl of his choosing. They were quite taken aback when they brought up the subject of marriage and Debashish told them that the only kind of wife that he could live with was the obedient, shy, naïve, inquisitive, ambitionless, and strikingly beautiful Indian kind. His parents, having been born and brought up in India, suggested to him that the concept of Indians in the minds of Canadian desis was something other than the concept of Indians in the minds of Indians. Thus it was a most curious trio of Deshpandes that entered the Verma residence that day. There was papa Deshpande, mama Deshpande, and Debashish Deshpande on the one sofa, and papa Verma, mama Verma, Amrita Verma, Ashok Verma, and Aparna Verma on the other.

It must be noted that the Verma residence was not the first to receive the Deshpandes as suitors. Neither were the Deshpandes the first to come knocking at the Verma door with a *rishtaa*. Both Amrita and Debashish had been through their share of meetings set up for the purpose of discussing an arranged marriage, and owing to their particular singularities, were still attending these meetings. The people were different, but the conversations were always the same.

Guy: Hi.
Girl: Hi.
Guy: This is kind of embarrassing, isn't it?
Girl: Yeah, kind of.
Guy: This is so stupid. Can you believe that we're still being forced to do this? I mean, it's the twenty-first century, for God's sake.
Girl: I know. How can they expect us to live under the same rituals that they lived with thirty years ago? I'm just doing this because I have no choice. I have to listen to what my parents say.
Guy: Yeah, same here. I mean they do love us and they're only doing what they think is best for us.
Girl: Yeah.
Guy: Yeah. So do you have a boyfriend?
Girl: No. You? A girlfriend, I mean.
Guy: Well, I had many in my college days, but now I have a job and I just want to settle down with someone.
Girl: Yeah, okay.
Guy: Yeah. Listen I had something to ask you, kind of personal actually.
Girl: Yeah, me too.
Guy: Okay, you go first.
Girl: No, no, you go first.
Guy: Ladies first.
Girl: No, you mentioned it first.
Guy: Okay fine, at the same time.
Girl: Okay.
Guy: Ready, set, go.
Guy and Girl: Are you a virgin?

This was where most arranged marriages were made or unmade. The truth was seldom told by either party, and it was never so much the actual answer to the question as much as the impression created from

Ignatius J.

the dialogues that followed the asking of the question that determined the course for two marriage-aged desis. Either both parties involved were open to compromises, or at least one of them had a preexisting opinion on the question. It was precisely their own concepts of the question that had prevented Amrita and Debashish from fulfilling the penultimate obligation that every desi has to his or her parents.

In the living room of the Verma house regular *baath-cheeth* was exchanged between papa Deshpande and papa Verma and between mama Deshpande and mama Verma. Debashish, Amrita, Ashok, and Aparna stared attentively at their reflections in the coffee cups in their hands.

Papa Deshpande: See, Mr Verma, we have a saying back in Canada. There is no "I" in team. What that means is that Sachin Tendulkar cannot be expected to do the work of ten other cricketers.

Mama Verma: *Chi, chi*, you went to that store. I wouldn't wear the saris from that store even to my enemy's wedding. Don't worry; when this is all fixed, I'll take you to my special store.

Papa Verma: The way I see it, everyone who immigrated is regretting it. They call me and you know what they say? Ey, Verma, you were right *yaar*. My wife walks around wearing skirts and drinking at bars and if I tell her anything she says she'll divorce me and ask for alimony. Anything I say to my children they say they'll arrest me for child abuse.

Mama Deshpande: Did you hear? I think Akshay and Twinkle are breaking up. They were so cute together. But I knew it when I saw *Kuch Kuch Nahin Ho Raha Hai* that something was going on between Twinkle and Bobby.

It was after ten minutes of this kind of conversation that papa Deshpande rather humourously suggested that Amrita and Debashish were probably getting bored. The parents laughed loudly, the children nervously. Papa Verma added that perhaps the children had something to talk about on their own. He suggested that Amrita show Debashish her room.

Debashish: Hi.
Amrita: Okay, let's cut the bullshit, okay?

Debashish: Uh, okay.

Amrita: Sorry I snapped. It's just that most of the NRIS want a servile virgin housewife who moonlights as a whore, depending on her husband's mood. What are *you* looking for?

Debashish: I came here looking for something else and when I got here I think I started wanting something else. I don't really know anymore. I thought I wanted some shy, naïve girl that I could show the whole world to, but now I feel like everyone here has seen more of the world than me.

Amrita: I don't mean to sound rude, but if you don't know what you're looking for, shouldn't you first figure that out, and then go looking? I mean, this is just wasting both our time, isn't it?

Debashish: Yeah, I guess so. Listen, I think I like you. Can I take you out to a movie or for a drink or something?

Amrita: Okay, sure. But don't go falling in love with me or anything just yet. Before anything else, I want to know how good you are in bed.

Debashish: Really? Oh, okay. I'm a virgin.

The next day, Debashish was not a virgin. The night before, the first thing Debashish did upon returning home, well past his normal bedtime, was to make a long distance call to his desi colleague and friend in Toronto.

Debashish: What's up, dude?

Friend: Hey, man, you got a wife yet?

Debashish: Not yet. But I got laid, man.

Friend: Who was it this time? Your right hand or your left hand?

Debashish: Neither, man. This is the real deal. It was this girl I was supposed to marry.

Friend: No way! An Indian girl? Did you pay in Canadian or Indian? Remind me never to drink from the same glass as you again.

Debashish: Shut up, man. It actually happened, okay?

Friend: Shit! You're serious? What was it like? Did it hurt?

Debashish: No, of course not. I mean, maybe a bit. But it was so cool, man. But then, it didn't last too long.

Friend: How long did you go for, you stud?

Debashish: I'd say we went for a good one-and-a-half minutes.

Friend: No way! You mean you PMEd while PMsing?
Debashish: What?
Friend: You had a premature ejaculation while having premarital sex, man. Shit, I told you that you need to masturbate more, *na*?

STORY THE SECOND

Ignatius J. had just gotten off the phone with his friend and ex-partner-in-virginity. While he was happy for his friend's good fortunes, he did at the same time feel lonely all of a sudden. His only release was his favourite Canadian Indians chat service that he promptly logged on to.

Chat moderator: Iggystud69 has logged in.
SexyShahrukh: Hey Kajol2o, are you a whore?
Iggystud69: Hi everybody. Hey girls, anyone want to have some innocent friendship and fun?
Kajol2o: Go fuck yourself SexyShahrukh.
Chat Moderator: Aishwarya19 has logged in.
SexyShahrukh: Hey Aishwarya19, are you a whore?
Iggystud69: Hey Aishwarya19. Just ignore SexyShahrukh. He's a bastard.
Desipoet: God, are all Indian guys except me such pathetic, immature losers? Hey, any girls out there who want to have intellectual discussions only, just pm me.
KrazyKumar: Hi Aishwarya19. Do you look like Aishwarya Rai?
AwesomeAkshay: No girls should send private messages to Desipoet. He is a fat, ugly loser. Hey Aishwarya19. Hey Kajol2o. Hey, all girls. Where are you all? Don't be so shy and quiet.
TheVoice: Hey Iggy, what's up, man?
Desilicious: Hey, any boys want to have some fun?
Desidude: Hey Desilicious, I want some fun. You sound delicious. And Desi. Lol.
AwesomeAkshay: Hi Desilicious. A/s/l?
SexyShahrukh: Hey Desilicious, are you a whore?
KrazyKumar: Hey Aishwarya19. You didn't answer my question. Do you look like Aishwarya Rai?

Chat Moderator: Desipoet has logged out.

Iggystud69: Hey guys, Desilicious is a guy. Trust me, he was here yesterday asking if any boys wanted to have some fun. He's a fag. Hey TheVoice, my friend just lost his virginity, man. I'm so pissed off. I want to lose my virginity also. Hey, any girls want to fuck a virgin? Any girls from Toronto here?

Desilicious: Hi Desidude. I like your style. Hi AwesomeAkshay. I'm 20/female/Ottawa. Hi SexyShahrukh, I can be your whore if you want me to. Lol. Hey Iggystud69, there's a reason you're still a virgin.

Chat Moderator: Desipoet has logged in.

Chat Moderator: BigDesiDick has logged in.

Chat Moderator: Desidame has logged in.

AwesomeAkshay: Hey Desilicious, do you have a pic? Hi Desidame.

SexyShahrukh: Hey Desidame, are you a whore?

BigDesiDick: Any ladies looking for some brown action? I am qualified instructor in *Kama Sutra* straight from India. I can teach all 99 variations, including the complicated Praying Mantis position and the nearly impossible Flustered Peacock position. Any takers? This is the real deal ladies. Not some Canadian copy. If any of you are coming to India you definitely want to feel the desi touch of bigdesidick before you go back to your boring lives. Come on, anyone?

TheVoice: Hey Iggy. Fuck your friend, man. So what if he's gone over to the dark side. We're still here, man. Fight the temptation.

Desidame: Hi everybody. Hi AwesomeAkshay. Anyone here seen *Dimag tho pagal hai?*

Iggystud69: Hey Desidame. Yeah, I saw that movie. It was too good. Are you in Toronto?

Desipoet: Hey any girls here read any Kafka? Shakespeare? Rushdie? Roy? Most of the guys here are so sex-crazed. It's the problem with the whole Indian culture. Sex is seen as so taboo so they come here and just make fools of themselves and give our country a bad name. They are using their anonymity to vent their sexual frustrations instead of being mature and sophisticated. Hey any smart girls in here who want to talk about geopolitics vis-a-vis Kashmir?

Chat Moderator: BigDesiDick has logged out.

Chat Moderator: Iggystud69 has logged out.

Anwar Sadaf got the call just as he had logged off from seven different Indian chat services in three continents. He often felt that Delhi was too small for him.

Amrita: Hey, you big desi dick.

Anwar: Hey. Nothing against the lovely nickname you've given me; I'm actually quite proud of it, but I do have a real name. It's Anwar.

Amrita: Really, well, that doesn't interest me. To me you're just big desi dick.

Anwar: Glad to know how I measure up with you. So how's your super stud suitor boy doing?

Amrita: He's probably masturbating furiously, trying to make up for two decades of abstinence.

Anwar: Maybe next time he'll make the four-minute mark. Who knows, he may even go on for a full five minutes. That's a whole hand to count on.

Amrita: Hey, don't make fun of my potential husband. Only I have the right to do that. I think I like him. He obviously needs a lot of work in the bedroom department. But I think he'll work that out and I'll be there to help him. He asked me to go to a movie called *Dilwali Dulha Le Jayegi* with him. I think I'll go. I like talking to him. He thinks I'm sincere and honest. At least he doesn't think of me purely as a sperm receptacle.

Anwar: You know what, that hurts. I would never describe our relationship as being purely sexual. It has its platonic moments. Few and far between as they may be, it is the quality and not the quantity that makes the difference.

Amrita: Yeah, yeah, stop jabbering. Thank you so much for coming on such short notice last night, by the way. I was just in the mood for a long night and after the short sprint to the finish line from my man formerly known as a virgin, it was either you or my vibrator. Truth be told, I didn't particularly care which it was. Lucky for you, the phone was closer.

Anwar: It's nice to know that at such moments of depraved desperation you think of the big desi dick. Listen, I would love to continue this phone sex session with you but I'm expected at the Dance bar.

Amrita: Well, cancel your plans. You're coming to the clinic with me tonight.

Anwar: No, that is not fair. You said you would go alone. We discussed this last night.

Amrita: That was post-orgasm. I'm too nice post-orgasm. Now either you're coming with me and enjoying the benefits of our arrangement until the arrangement of my marriage, or you can go back to your neglected right hand. What will it be?

Anwar: Hell hath no fury.

Amrita: That's right, darling.

Anwar had to delay his meeting at the Dance bar in order to take Amrita to the local private clinic.

Anwar: You're asking for it. Not me.

Amrita: I asked for it last night, you ask for it tonight.

Anwar: Asking for sex is different from asking for the morning-after pill. I'm a guy, for god's sake. I can't go in there and ask for the pill.

Amrita: Is it just me or does your right hand look particularly rough and dry tonight? You should get some moisturizer.

Anwar: Fine, but I'm not paying for it. You are.

Amrita: You broke it, you pay for it.

Anwar: Come on, its not like I broke the condom on purpose. Ah, what's the point of arguing?

Amrita: There is none, sweetie.

Anwar managed to buy the morning-after pill without receiving too many amused stares in return. After a quickie in the back seat *sans* condom, he dropped Amrita home and made off for the Dance bar. He was an hour late when he got to the seedy hangout for Delhi's sexually frustrated middle-class. The Dance bar functioned as a restaurant and a bar, but what it was most famous for was the line of prostitutes clad in crisp white saris dancing to catchy Bollywood tunes on a stage in the middle of the restaurant. The air inside, not at all like the air outside, was composed mainly of cigarette smoke, with trace amounts of oxygen. Anwar made his way down the dimly lit aisle separating the tables that were next to the walls and completely in the dark from the stage that had disco lights alternating between blue, green, red, and yellow. He found his friend at one of the larger tables with a couple of strangers.

Friend: Hey, you finally made it, man. How did it go with your sweetheart?

Anwar: Don't ask, man. And she's not my sweetheart.

Stranger 1: I like that one with the long straight black hair.

Friend: Come on, man, tell her you love her and get it over with.

Stranger 2: They all have long straight black hair. I like that one with the large breasts.

Anwar: She's probably getting married in a week. I don't even know if I really want to marry her. I mean I love having sex with her, but we haven't really talked much about anything besides sex. I don't even think she sees me as anything more than a vibrator with a large bank balance.

Stranger 1: They all have large breasts. Are you sure you want to do this?

Friend: Well then, fuck her and forget about it. Come on, pick a girl. It's on me.

Stranger 2: Yeah, I'm pretty sure. I think.

Anwar: Thanks for the offer. I'll take it up next time I'm here. I've already filled up my quota for tonight. You pick, I'll pay.

Stranger 1: Okay, so just pick a girl and go do whatever you have to do.

Friend: Feeling generous? It must be the post-orgasm effect. I like that one with the long straight black hair.

Stranger 2: Look, I want you to understand why I am doing this. I just lost my virginity to a girl I might marry in a week. I don't want to spend the rest of married life with a complex over all the guys my wife has laid. I want to know what different women are like. How they scream, how they moan, what they like, what they don't like – I want to know everything about sex before I decide to spend the rest of my life having sex with the same girl.

Anwar: They all have long straight black hair. I like that one with the large breasts.

174 ~

Temptress

KAREEMA BESH

At the age of five, I started attending Sunday school in the *masjid*. Scarf covering my hair, legs swinging, every Sunday I sat and listened to the Sisters talk about Allah, and Mohammed, and how to be a Good Muslim.

Even then I knew that was what my parents wanted me to be. A Good Muslim. Because education, a good job, speaking fluent Urdu, none of it really mattered if you weren't a Good Muslim. But my brain had been coated with anti-goodness Teflon, and none of the morality the Sisters would try and teach us in Sunday school would stick. It soon became obvious to me that I was never meant to be good.

Once I raised my hand in class and asked why boys didn't have to wear *hijab* and cover their heads like girls did.

"Because," said Sister Amna, "that is what the Qu'ran says."

"But what's the reason for it?"

Sister Amna gave me a weary look. "Women cover their heads to be modest and so they do not tempt men."

"But why does the Qu'ran make women cover their heads? Why doesn't it make men behave themselves and not be tempted?"

Sister Amna ignored my question.

That day I learned that I was not simply Nina, a thirteen-year-old Pakistani Muslim, but Nina, a thirteen-year-old Pakistani Muslim temptress, possessing within me a beauty so strong and sexual that if I uncovered myself men would be left powerless by their own lust. If I took my scarf off, I would render men useless, so overwhelmed with desire they would be unable to function. Now, when I sat in my Sunday school class, I longed to take my scarf off and swing it around my head madly and watch all the boys fall to their knees, eyes tearing with desire.

That same year I got my period and my parents began to treat me differently. Those sleepovers I used to go to at my non-Muslim friends' houses were now forbidden. I wasn't allowed to go to the school dances. The clothing I wore received much more scrutiny – this shirt was too tight, that skirt revealed too much ankle. My mother kept asking me, her eyes suspicious, if any of my friends had boyfriends. I lied and said no. Although I didn't have a boyfriend, many of my friends did. I think my scarf kept boys away. To them, I was different, untouchable. I drew great satisfaction in knowing that if I took off my hijab in front of them, they would all go mad for me, carry my books, ask me to dances, do anything to get close enough to touch my temptress skin.

But I kept my scarf on and my sexual power hidden. My teenage years were passing uneventfully, my life strictly controlled by my parents, who lived in constant fear of my corruption by immoral Western ideas. I turned sixteen, a prom came and went, and I stayed at home, wishing I could have just a small taste of a man, never imagining I would find it where I least expected.

~

In Islam, women always pray behind the men. In our *masjid*, the women had their own balcony, and prayed above and behind the men. I was told that this is because if women prayed in front of men, men would be too distracted at the sight of women's bodies in front of them, motioning up and down, their round buttocks slicing through the air as they prostrated before Allah. I never understood why women and men couldn't pray side by side. I supposed even this would be too tempting, as a stealthy sideways glance would allow a man to see our breasts hanging down as we placed our hands on our knees – dozens of pairs of temptress breasts, dangling like branches from a weeping willow, all in a row.

One Sunday, walking into the *masjid*, I caught Hassan's eye. Hassan was my age. He was one of the tallest boys at the *masjid* and had been coming there almost as long as I had. He had dark brown hair and eyes, which created an alluring contrast with his fair skin. Hassan half-smiled at me and then quickly looked away. I found myself blushing, cheeks hot.

After class there was always a recess, during which all of the kids would go outside and hang out in the parking lot, boys on one side, girls on another. All of the teenage girls would stand around in small groups and talk about movie stars, shopping, and boys, until a sister stuck her head out and yelled for us to come in.

On this afternoon, like many others before it, our conversation centred on boys. "Who do you think the hottest guy is?" Khadija asked.

"Hassan," replied Mona.

"Hassan? He's not all that," I said, a little too quickly.

"Did you hear about Brother Jaffer?" someone asked. Brother Jaffer was a Sunday school teacher who was very active in the *masjid* administration. He was tall and had a neatly trimmed beard. He yelled at me once because my scarf had fallen too far back on my head. ("Do not forget you are in the house of Allah," he wagged his finger at me. "How can I?" I had muttered under my breath.)

Someone else chimed in. "Yeah, he just got married to some girl who's eighteen." Brother Jaffer was over forty.

"Yuck," I said.

"So?" Yasmin said. "I'm going to get married when I'm eighteen."

"To someone who's forty?" I asked.

"Who cares?" Yasmin countered. "I'll be having s-e-x before any of you."

The younger girls giggled at the word, and no one had a reply. I pictured pretty Yasmin at eighteen being kissed by a bearded old man, his wrinkled hands stroking her soft cheeks. Just then the *adhan* bellowed out from the speakers, and we started to file back inside.

During prayer, the *imam* recited vaguely familiar verses in Arabic and my mind wandered. I looked down at the men sitting below, trying to spot Hassan in the sea of backs, no small feat considering the amount of black-haired heads below. I managed to find him, in the corner, and watched him during the rest of the prayer. Watched him go up, go down, watched the curve of his pants around his buttocks grow tight and then slack again as he bent down and stood up. Hassan turned his head slightly and made eye contact with me, as if he had heard my thoughts. Embarrassed, I looked downward at my hands, which were trembling.

It happened like that the next four Sundays. We would make brief eye contact in the halls, and then during prayer he would always look back at me, just once, just for a second. I always prayed in the same place so it was easier to find me, and he did the same. But we never spoke to each other, and maintained our distance.

One night, I had a dream. I was praying and Hassan looked back at me as usual. But this time he stood up and walked towards me. He was able to walk on air and he came right up to the balcony where I sat. We looked at each other for a moment, and then he reached his hand out and in one deft move undid my scarf. My long black hair fell down my back and he grabbed it in his hands, twisting it around in his fingers. Then he started kissing it, kissed each strand one by one. I woke up suddenly, a few beads of sweat on my brow, my body quivering, and was unable to fall asleep again.

I was late the next Sunday because I had tried to convince my mother that morning that I shouldn't have to go to *masjid* anymore, as I had learned everything I need to know to be a Good Muslim. But the more I pressed it, the more determined my mother was to force me to go. As I walked toward the entrance, I saw Hassan standing on the stairs, talking to a friend. Class had already started, and I wondered if Hassan was planning on skipping.

As I got closer, I wondered what to do. Ignore him? Smile? Maybe even dare to offer a barely perceptible wink? I adjusted my scarf and took a deep breath. I would give him a quick smile, I decided, and move along.

But when I walked by, he didn't look at me. I floated by unnoticed, or so I thought, until someone behind me pressed something into my hand. I looked back, but Hassan had already slid past me and was walking towards his classroom. No one else was around, so I opened the note. "Look for me during break, and follow me – if you want to. Hassan." There it was, on the back of an old lotto ticket, a literal acknowledgement that the looks we shared every week meant something beyond mere casual glances induced by boredom. I knew I shouldn't go, shouldn't take the first step down the slippery slope of teenage trysts, and with a boy from the *masjid*, of all places! But my body was already betraying my head by tingling in anticipation, and I knew I would obey his instructions.

Class had never seemed so slow, and when it ended I rushed outside, hoping to avoid running into anyone. I saw Hassan in a corner of the parking lot, and he nodded at me and started walking away from the *masjid*. I followed him, a good pace behind. There were a couple of acres of woods behind the *masjid*, where it was rumoured that some of the kids would sneak out and have a smoke. I doubted many did, as most kids would rather wait until they left to have a smoke than come back to prayer smelling of it and get admonished by Brother Jaffer. I was confident we wouldn't run into anyone, and this confidence pushed me forward, deeper into the woods, until I could hardly see the *masjid*. Hassan leaned against a tree, smiling.

"I wasn't sure if you would come," he said.

"Me either," I responded.

He sat down on a rock and offered me the other one. "It's funny, I've known you for years and we've never really talked."

"Yeah, well," I grinned, "the *masjid* isn't exactly a great place to get to know members of the opposite sex."

We talked for a while. I learned that he played guitar, but his father didn't like him to play it too much in case he got it in his head to run away and become a rock star. Hassan told his father he was writing songs in praise of Islam, like Cat Stevens did now, but really they were about death and sadness.

"Do you ever perform them?" I asked.

Hassan shrugged. "Not really. Sometimes, my mom will stand outside my door and listen. She thinks I don't know."

"Sing one for me," I asked.

He sang it for me in his sweet, young voice. "Every Sunday our eyes met/and said what our mouths couldn't say/do you think she could ever love me/that girl seems so far away."

My teenage ears had never heard anything so beautiful. I was blushing madly; I could feel it. An incredible rush coursed through my veins – a boy liked me. A boy liked *me*. And I liked him back.

"Would you mind if I kissed you?" he asked.

I wasn't sure how to kiss, so I let him guide me. His lips pressed against mine and I felt his tongue requesting entrance, so I let it in. His tongue was warm and when it touched mine I started to breath faster, the thoughts left my mind and all I knew was his tongue and his skin and my hands on my shoulders.

Hassan suddenly pulled away. "We missed the prayer," he said, slightly out of breath.

"Oh," I said, not caring, just wanting to kiss him again. "No one will miss us."

"We have to get back," Hassan said. "You should go first. You know the back door, next to. . . ."

"I can handle it," I said and started to walk away.

Hassan grabbed my arm. "Next Sunday."

I wasn't sure if this was a question or a statement, but I wholeheartedly agreed. I was beginning to understand what my parents and the Sisters and everyone was trying to hide from me – the thrill of making out with a boy, the intensity that you never want to end. But Sister Amna was wrong. I was not only a temptress, I could also be tempted by another. I was not just a passive vessel for someone else's desire. I had my own desire, and plenty of it.

So our Sunday schedule began. Sometimes we would only spend a short time in the woods so we could return in time for prayer, sometimes we would miss prayer altogether. I became very familiar with his tongue, how it moved, how to flirt with it. Time passed, and one day the fervent groping ran its natural progression to him unbuttoning my shirt. I hesitated, and then he pulled my bra down, and soon my shirt was off.

It may have been a funny picture, a couple in the woods, the girl wearing a head scarf but no shirt, pressing a boy's mouth to her breast, eyes half-closed, lips slightly parted. But if it was, I didn't notice, and didn't care.

Of course, I then made him reciprocate. His chest was broad, with a line of soft hair growing down the middle. His stomach was flat and strong, and I would often lean my head against it. We talked about our dreams. I wanted to go to college some place very far away from my parents, and he wanted to be a songwriter and a mechanic. He worked with a mechanic after school and figured his dreams should be tempered by doses of realism.

Months went by and our Sunday afternoon rendezvous continued. I think a few people were beginning to notice our simultaneous absence, but no one said anything. As one of the oldest teenagers still coming to the *masjid*, I was now a teaching assistant, helping the young boys and the girls memorize their *suras* and read the Qu'ran. My favourite class was the one where we told the children stories about the lives of Muhammed and all of the other prophets. I would teach the children about Prophet Sulaiman, who could talk to birds, and Prophet Yunus, who lived inside a whale, and then I would sneak off to the woods to be in the arms of Hassan, lessons of the prophets forgotten in an embrace.

Winter came and we huddled in the woods, lips locked, using each other for heat. The frost in the air limited us to roaming hands beneath clothing and getting into snow fights when we got bored, trying to not to shout lest someone hear us.

So we rejoiced when the snow finally melted and the leaves grew back to hide our bodies from view. One afternoon as we lay there in silence, Hassan said, "You know, I've never really seen your hair."

"Well, you've never taken my scarf off," I said. I looked at him. "Why haven't you?"

"I don't know. It was easier to take your shirt off," he laughed.

"So, do you want to see?" I asked.

"Of course."

"Are you sure you're ready?"

He looked at me quizzically. "Ready for what?"

"I'm not sure." I paused, and then untied my scarf, tossing my hair around to get rid of my scarf-head.

Hassan looked at me for a second, no doubt storing the image of when he first saw me with my hair rolling down my shoulders in the back of his mind for posterity. He sat up and stroked my hair gently. "You're so beautiful," he said, and kissed me.

We clung to each other for a long time that day.

"You know this will end soon," he said.

"Why?" I asked, thinking he meant because I was leaving soon. I was going to Pakistan for the summer with my family, and starting college soon after that. "You know I'm only going to college three hours away." My parents, encouraged by my studiousness at school and eagerness to teach at the *masjid*, had agreed to let me go to a college in the neighbouring state in the fall.

"I know," he said and took my hand.

But the gesture was empty, and I realized what he really meant. Our entire relationship consisted of less than a half-hour together, hidden from the world, one day a week. I would go to college and my Sunday afternoons would be spent with people I didn't even know yet. The end of us was unavoidable, and approaching fast. But as our last remaining Sundays passed, we spoke nothing of it, like two people on the shore silently waiting for the tide to come in and wash away their footprints. Finally there was a passionate goodbye, a few quiet tears, and it ended as covertly as it began, in the woods, under the cover of trees.

~

In one of the Sunday school classes, I had taught the children the story of Prophet Yusuf. His was one of the more entertaining stories to teach, rife with scheming brothers and prison sentences. In the story, Zulaikha is the wife of the rich Egyptian minister who took in the excruciatingly handsome Yusuf. Every day she watches the angel-like Yusuf eat, sleep, walk, and talk, and is beside herself with desire. But Yusuf, being a Good Muslim, rejects her passionate advances. For this, she has him imprisoned, but not before she invites all of the women to her house. As the women slice fruit, she presents them with Yusuf to prove how irresistibly tempting he is, and overcome with lust and longing at the sight of him, the women cut their hands with their knives, warm blood dripping from their fingers, staining the whites of the apple slices a deep red.

After I left Hassan and Sundays at the *masjid*, I knew I would never be one of those women, standing there with cut and bloody hands, full of frustrated desires. I would embrace my sexuality, not be ashamed of it. Men would fall at my feet, yearn for my lips and my caresses, my round breasts and black hair. They would succumb to my temptations, and I to theirs. And one day, I hoped, I would meet a man who would tempt me forever.

I never saw Hassan again. But even now, so many years later, I still think of him. I picture him in my daydreams, lying in the woods, red and gold leaves caught in his hair, kissing my neck as he twists my hair around his fingers, just us and the sun and the squirrels, and, in the background, the call to prayer from the *masjid* loudspeaker filtering though the trees, bittersweet music to our ears.

The Secret Life of Good Boys

SANDIP ROY

Electric shock from bruised grass as you wrestle around. Schoolboy knees touching on hard wooden benches. A sudden shock of armpit hair as the school football captain yanks off his jersey. First shadow of a moustache on a schoolmate. Groping behind a tree on warm monsoon nights. A much-pirated blue movie – the sex scenes jumping and streaky as if they have been played on slow one too many times. Urgent sweaty sex before the maidservant got back from the market. Feeling a man rub up against you on a crowded train – a heady mix of Old Spice and sweat. The coppery play of the muscles on the back of a young man bathing at a tube well on the street. The rasp of a lover's chin and the taste of cigarettes on his tongue. A stolen vacation up in the hills – a massage under covers after a day of horseback riding. Pretending to pee in the park so he can reach over and touch you.

Growing up in India, gay sex was stolen, grabbed, seized whenever I could. Everything had to somehow fall in place – parents had to be out of the house, the servants needed to be gone, brothers and sisters needed to be at their friends'. Even then there was no respite. Aunts could drop by without notice. Neighbours were curious why you had the windows closed at eight in the evening.

I didn't even know where to find it. I was the proverbial "good boy" in school, my lack of interest in girls held up like a medal of honour by the parents of my schoolmates. I was the one who would be sent to the parents' as proof that we wouldn't be up to any mischief while they were away for the evening. So could they please leave the TV room unlocked? Of course, as soon as they were gone, my friends would smuggle in the porn tape they had pooled their money to rent at some exorbitant price from the neighbourhood porn*walla*. I dutifully contributed my ten rupees to the pool though the grainy tape of bouncing breasts and ugly men didn't do anything for me.

I wondered if the porn*walla* had figured out that the European magazines I got from him were all the ones that had hard-bodied lean men alongside the women. (They didn't stock any gay porn at all, though the occasional bi one slipped through.) Once I had paid for it, if I wasn't carrying a bag, I'd stick it under the front of my shirt and smuggle it into the house, walking very slowly so it wouldn't slip out. Then a week later I'd sell it back to him for less than half the price. By then I'd decided I needed to stop wasting money. But he would say, "I have some new ones from Germany," and go behind the stack of musty old books and retrieve them from his stash. He also had porn written in Hindi and Bengali. The little books were covered in lurid yellow plastic and the pictures looked like horrible photocopies from some foreign magazine. But what captivated me was the text. Well brought up good boy that I was, I hardly knew what the words meant. Someone just went overboard writing those books – every sound in the sex act was recorded there. Reading them filled me with a weird secret sense of revulsion like I was stepping into another world that was guttural and dirty. At the same time it filled me with awe that my mother tongue Bengali that I knew through exquisite refined poems in my textbooks could be so filthy and hardcore.

Cruising in parks had to be timed exquisitely. The window of opportunity was small. Between occasional patrolling cops looking for a bribe and a need-to-be-back-home-by-9:30-for-dinner deadline, you didn't have much time to waste. If he looked acceptable, if there was no one around, you would be a fool to waste the opportunity. If the lights went out in the neighbourhood, as they did every other day, the boys in the park would make the most of their sudden privacy. Instantly shapes appeared behind trees. Men sitting next to each other casually touched hands, a finger crawling under your palm to lightly stroke it. We went to empty bus depots at night to have sex on the top decks of double-decker buses that were garaged there.

"Remember my name is Shovon," said my friend Sumit before we entered the twilight world of park cruising. We all had different names there, vague addresses; "I live over there." We were always paranoid someone would see us, that some friend of your father's on an evening walk would come across you. But in our secret shadowy world, people knew each other and looked out for each other. If they hadn't seen someone in a while they worried about him. "His wife must be keeping him busy," laughed someone. They would wander down the paths together, teasing each other with snatches of song, their cigarettes bobbing along. All of them, all us waiting for the park to quiet down, for night to fall before we took someone behind the bushes. Now and then a fish jumped from the water with a plop. Across the lake we could see the clubhouse – the lights glittering and the laughter and talk of the club-goers wafting across the water like smoke. It seems romantic in retrospect, but at that time it was anything but romantic. It was fast and hurried, it was a fumbling dance of zippers and belts, it was scary, it was dangerous – exposing ourselves to cops, thugs, blackmail, and AIDS.

At that time, we would long for languorous sex. When we could do it on our own beds. When we could fall asleep in each other's arms and wake up to the sunlight streaming over our tangled bodies . . . and then do it again. Our beds. Our place. No need to worry about parents, brothers, nosy neighbours, visiting aunts. We'd dream about bars where we could cruise at leisure. No need to hurry as if they would yank the buffet away any minute.

The first time I got that after moving to America, I was thrilled beyond belief. Your own bed. On your own terms. Your handpicked man. The first time I brought a man home from the bar, the sex was almost secondary. The excitement, the thrill was just bringing him home and turning the key in the lock. It was my own private revolution.

But funnily, even the thrill became routine, almost too convenient, domestic. Not forbidden anymore. We didn't have to do it right here, right now. We could always do it tomorrow or the day after. The bars with their drink specials and the clubs with the Ecstasied-out shirtless boys twirling in the haze of the fog machines, the sweat glistening on their perfect pecs, soon started feeling like I was trapped in a loop of someone else's gay fantasy. The prerequisite pre-sex pre-pickup banter of "Wow, do they have gay bars in India?" started getting old.

Sometimes it seemed easier to forget the flirting and the banter and just go to the bathhouse. "A bathhouse," my gay friends in India would sigh enviously. Here we could pay our ten dollars and walk around a bathhouse in a towel, two condoms and a sachet of lube laid out neatly on your pillow. And the attendants with white gloves came by as each person left and stripped the beds. It was a twenty-four-hour sex factory. Little monitors to tell you when your room was ready, or your time was up. Signs about HIV tests and warnings about syphilis. Everything humming along with ruthless efficiency. Sometimes I'd just stand and watch the white sheets go round and round in the big washers and marvel at where I was.

But sometimes I have the oddest hankering for that hurried fumble in the park, the unpredictability, the fillip of danger, that smell of bruised grass and spilled semen. Then we'd wipe up with that neatly folded cotton handkerchief all well-bred Indian schoolboys carried. And go back to our good-boy lives, convinced everyone could smell our bad-boy deeds.

Glebe Love Poems

ASOKA WEERASINGHE

I

I wasn't going to
love you the first
afternoon we met,
but when I saw
the form of the pink crevice
cushioned heavenly in silver-down
between your soft thighs,
I wanted to separate its lips
with a thrust of my body
with the innocence of a younger
immigrant from the Orient
for you to love it
humping with your body.
I swear you were amazing
for a grandmother at 65.

2

At falling in love
eyes, palms, and what else.
You have all I need to
fall for you,
a shaven cunt
the tattoo of a rose
on a rounded buttock-cheek
and lips that I could eat.

~ 187

All what I just wanted
last week on a 65-year-old
senior so long ago.
I thought, no doubt, some day
a senior will have the desire
to stroke an Oriental ebony-dark
night shaft, switch its light on
and fall in love.

3

The temple of your vintage body
is the holy house for the younger lover
dignified in the exploding darkness
with a bronze spike of Oriental flesh
where he tongues feverishly
your custard-layered altar.

4

I will give you all tonight
the first of four consecutive nights
even though your hairs
are silvered with age
with my shield, my sword,
gilded in molten bronze
standing erect, which is my dream.
My strength is to pierce between
the valley of your moons,
the first of two-thousand-and-five-
hundred non-stop thrusts. And tonight
I shall give you my very life
with the mango perfumed tip
of the sword. I will give you all tonight.

5

Lying on my back
you swoop over me
like a red-tailed hawk.
I see the red of your eyes
the beak in your lips
and the broad wings spreading
from your voluptuous hips.
In a moment of lust
you swoop on the bronzed stake
turned warm flesh,
your talons the fingers
of your eager palm
plucking it into your throat.
The tingling mesh of my mind
is webbed in your silver hair
and the night-pink of your body
that I embrace.

Asoka Weerasinghe

Polishing My Skin

NAZNEEN SHEIKH

They have come for me. Two women carrying wicker baskets covered with cloth and a small charcoal brazier. My mother and sisters have left. All my mother whispered into my ear was, "Let them prepare you." This time it is a gentle entreaty, quite unlike her usual stern maternal injunctions. This time her gaze softens as she strokes back the strands of hair sculpted across my forehead. I am startled because in the shining depths of her brown eyes I see the iris ringing out as though it is trying to contain something that smoulders . . . unfurls inside. I have never seen this expression in my mother's eyes before, and I move closer to her, but she has turned away and moves beyond the door. I am left with the two women who have already shut the door to the bathhouse in my grandmother's ancestral home.

The wedding is five hours away and the city of Lahore scorches under a July sun. Not here, though, in this plaster and tile room equipped with water faucets mounted above a tiled bathing trough. I have heard about this bathhouse since I was a child. All the women of the family have come here before their weddings to be "prepared." When they are viewed many hours later as brides, each one shimmers with an uncanny luminosity that we all know has nothing to do with cosmetics. No one shares the secret and nothing is ever discussed. Now it is my turn, and I can hardly wait. I am not like the other women. I am my mother's wayward daughter who has lived in the West and is not a virgin. The man I have chosen to marry is much older than me, and a Hispanic American. I have brought him to my father's home so we can have a traditional wedding. This is the land of soft women with hard yet resilient minds. So I am here not to indulge my mother but to satisfy my curiosity. My favourite aunt has guessed it, though; she looked at me with a diamond winking in her pierced nostril and said, "The West cannot teach you the mysteries of the East." Her comment is clichéd and outmoded, yet I am ensnared. I grew up surrounded by these women who had husbands chosen for them. Educated women, who managed to escape abroad for prized vacations with their husbands so that they could get their hair permed in Paris and pick up shoes in Rome. Their conversations were dotted with anecdotes of their husbands, children, tailors, and maidservants. Some of them held political debates and exercised intellectual freedom in unique ways, but they never spoke about sex or desire, let alone their orgasms, or their fantasies. It was their lot, I had decided, and nothing whatsoever to do with me. I had my hair cut at Vidal Sassoon and poured myself into denim and offered my body to men I desired. My only innate female vanity is to envelop myself in rose-scented fragrances.

The two women are busy removing objects from the baskets. The older one moves slowly, giving instructions to the younger one, who is plump and given to giggling. They are professionals in the rituals of their trade, which has been passed along from mother to daughter. The items they use are indigenous, organically grown, dried, and then pounded in a primitive mortar and pestle and finally stored in delicate earthenware vessels. I am told to remove my clothes. The older woman makes this request as casual as if she were asking for the time. The younger one pulls down a *charpai* that is leaning against one wall. It is the traditional hemp woven bed bolstered by four wooden legs. The legs are ornately carved and painted in lurid colours. As I step out of my clothes, the younger woman covers the bed with a white cotton sheet. I am naked in front of two other women who are fully clothed. The older woman looks at my body, and a smile plays across her lips. I am convinced she is taking some sort of inventory. Then she puts a hand on my shoulder and pivots me around. I almost stumble, but she holds my waist to steady me. The palms of her hand are soft, and I feel as though a silken sash is holding me in place. She is behind me now and I know that some sort of examination of my back is being conducted without my being touched. She steps out from behind me and leads me to bed. In that minute and a half I am made aware that some transformation of my body is imminent, and I instinctively trust my benefactress.

Silk, she says, looming over me, as I lie on the bed knotted with anticipatory tension, is always packed in tobacco leaves. But when we take it out, it is silk. I can make you into a river of silk and he will never want to cross to the other side. I will turn you into the milky flesh of the green almond, which he will hold in his mouth without ever swallowing. I can do without machines what they can never do in America. Amused, I gaze up at her face and nod. Then she deftly adds: It may hurt a little. Plump and giggling, Safia hands her strips of muslin coated with heated brown sugar and lemon juice. It starts from my ankles, the primitive depilatory process. The sticky heated embrace of the cloth, the quick caramelizing on the skin, and the sharp yank. A three-tiered process in which I go through a contracting, relaxing dance of my own. The discomfort is minimal. Silk and pearls, croons the woman, moving upward to my knees, deforesting my skin, making me truly naked. Defoliating, deforesting . . . denuding. Like some lyrical poetess, she hums with similes and metaphors. Then she takes my hand and trails the fingertips across one of my thighs. This is his hand, she whispers, these are his fingers. All you will have to do is look into his eyes and you will feel your own skin. I am instantly catapulted into the heavy-lidded gazes of Eastern men gazing from old portraits. Were all those smouldering orbs reflecting the opalescent skins of their hairless women? Was this the reason perhaps that women were hidden, veiled, and closeted from the eyes of men? How quickly would the warring instincts of their men be derailed by images of desire. All those pear-shaped Mughal women with complexions the colour of yellowing clotted cream had kept this secret buried. But I return again to this century and this room, where I sense that, although something else is about to begin, I am not certain if my hazel-eyed lover with his sensuous smile will attain the mystery of the East in his arms tonight.

Now this, she says, tapping my pubic mound, is like a ball of wool. What will he say when he gets here? There isn't any way to tell her how my soon-to-be husband separates with almost surgical delicacy all the strands of the ball of wool. How the anticipation of the moment as he deliberately prolongs finding my clitoral bud is also one of the more enthralling aspects of our lovemaking. You pant, he always chuckles, like a little animal. I say, record them, I want to hear these pants of mine. These half-breaths drawn out from my primeval self where I am neither human nor animal yet miraculously sensate. But a strip of muslin is already settling into place, and the following yank ricochets with a stinging pain that shocks me into silence. It is repeated three more times, and when it is over I discover a new sensorial receptor in my body. Now, says the woman, helping me up to a sitting position,

Desilicious

we will polish your skin. I glance down between my legs, seeing a continuous line of skin and the pale flesh rise of my pelvic mound a freshly revealed contour. I know I suddenly want a full-length mirror in order to pose for a moment like the heavy-hipped women of Botticelli and Titian.

Plump Safia's giggles hiccup softly in the room, and the gleam of approval mirrored in the older woman's eyes makes me rise slowly. I walk like a piece of statuary toward the bathing area. I walk like Cleopatra, Nefertiti, but most of all I walk like the Mughal Empress Nur Jehan, who hunted tigers and created Attar of Rose. I sit on the wooden stool placed in the sunken area near the taps, and as I reach towards a faucet, a hand encircles my wrist. It is the older woman, holding a clay jar in the crook of one arm. I am told to extend my arms and be still. There is more to come. The pale yellow paste is rubbed on my entire body and massaged vigorously. The base is turmeric, I am told. The other ingredients have names I cannot even pronounce. The supple movements of their fingers are circular. Both women work on my body as if they are polishing a metal object. I know for the first time how the skin folds over my elbow and how it disappears into a dimple behind my knee. How the spill of my stomach is guarded on either side by the angular thrust of my pelvic bones. Where the weight of my breasts create a niche in my midriff and how far my navel is embedded in my stomach. Every protrusion, each folded crevice is sought out and attended to.

Safia now turns on the water and collects it in a bucket, which she pours over my body. The older woman removes the paste with a coarse loofah. Each section of my cleaned body draws a satisfied murmur from the older woman, and I, suddenly gifted with this polished and tingling skin, am overwhelmed by the desire to rub myself like a cat against the fold of a curtain, the leg of a chair, and most of all the softly crisping hair on my lover's chest. My breasts begin to stiffen, and I cannot be certain if the liquid between my legs is water or my own juices. A heaviness, almost a languor, roots me to the wooden stool. When my feet are lifted one at a time and scrubbed with another paste, this one abrasive, I know that I will insist his tongue pay homage to every inch of this glistening nudity I call my body. When I am finished I feel ready to jump into a car and reach the hotel room, where he lies, waiting for his foreign wedding to begin. I don't want to cover myself with the stiff gold tissue outfit that has been stitched for me. I don't want the heavy, encrusted gold jewellery to pinch my throat and earlobes. I just want my nipples suckled into pellets and his sweet hard cock riding high inside me. I want the women not to disappear.

The older woman is rubbing my American shampoo into my wet hair. She sniffs at the mouth of the bottle once in curiosity and then again in obvious disdain. Yet she sees the warning in my eyes, so she works a lather in my hair. After Safia has poured the cool well water through it eight or nine times, I become aware of a hissing sound and a fragrance rising around us. It is coming from the small iron brazier that is lying close to one end of the bed. I inhale deeply, just the way you do with marijuana. It is sandalwood, pure with its almost sickly, sweet draw, coiling through the bathhouse. I am motioned toward the bed and told to lie down. Now, says the older woman, I will rub oil into your body; you will carry its fragrance through the first night into the second. I am eased up towards the edge of the bed so my hair hangs over the edge. Safia, positioned behind me on the floor, uses a fan to push the heated, fragrant smoke through my shoulder-length hair. Her fingers are parting my hair, coiling strands around and around. My head feels warm and cool simultaneously. I long to smell it, inhale the sandalwood, but I can't yet; the older woman is massaging my feet with slippery hands. Jasmine oil, she says to me. It is the lightest and the most delicate of all flowers. It is better in the heat, she adds. When you perspire, even your sweat will be scented.

Where is my lover, says my perfumed skin; I want him to ride me like a centaur in the heat of Lahore, pounding his haunches into mine, making me slippery with scented sweat. You will put it between your legs, yourself, she requests politely, this high priestess of flesh . . . this polisher of skin. Into my cupped palm she pours some oil, light as water, and I am dabbing between my legs around the lips, cautiously, towards the bud and then around the soft sides. I cannot go further because there is music pounding in my skull entirely made up of a palpitating state of desire. I want to escape this room and end this drawn-out erotic exercise where I have felt the power of my femininity only filtered through the ritual of this most exquisite of toilettes. This preparation which my mother had slipped into the chaos of my East/West marriage had been done only to remind me of the reverence paid to the act of love. Now the legions of Eastern women, shrouded by their stultifying conventions, assume a new aura for me. Their silence is understandable. They have memorized the ultimate sex manual, not with the aid of text or illustration but rather through the most conscious examination of their own bodies.

You, says the older woman, massaging my earlobes with jasmine oil, may wish to have something to drink. We give it to the younger brides. She had guessed, this polisher of skin, this titillater of nerve endings, that I had come back from the land of free and easy women. I am interested; I normally see things to the end. I sit up on the bed like a column of incense. Hair of sandalwood and body of jasmine, ready to swallow the libation of the moment. It is offered by Safia, who is giggling, in a metal glass. I am drinking milk with ground almonds, laced with powdered cardamom. It is cool, with a bit of an aftertaste. Nothing comes to mind. The older woman watches me intently. I drain the glass and wonder how much time has passed. Will anyone remember to collect me from this place? Safia brings the pile of fresh clothes for me to wear home. I am stepping into them slowly when I realize that my body has lost some contact with the outer edge of reality. I am floating in etherized form. There is no substance to my limbs as a series of minute explosions press out the unconscious tension that has always pulsed inside.

You are not even waiting now, whispers the older woman, as she leads me toward the door. You are in the moment, and what you have drunk heightens it so that it does not end even when you have taken him.

Much later, when a monsoon-like torrent cools the night and we lie in the flower-strewn debris of this great white bed and I am covered by the blanket of his limbs and he whispers, You are in my nostrils, in my hair . . . aah, the feel of you . . . I can hear the older woman wearing the face of Ikbal recite:

It must be known, this world of scent and sheen,
They must be plucked, the roses in the dene;
Yet do not close thine eyes upon the Self,
With thy soul a thing is to be seen.

~

I wrote this story because I wished to put women form the East and

West into the great white bed together. When the face of a Moroccan or Bengali woman peers out from a shrouded form, her sisters in Boston or Toronto conjure up images of deprivation and oppression. But the kaleidoscope needs to be tilted so that the celebration of erotic power is not stifled by geography. In the culture in which I was raised, the physical act of love becomes a form of worship, and at this altar the most glittering and precious offerings are our bodies.

Tattoo

RAJINDERPAL S. PAL

the bride sent back
the marriage annulled
for the blue of a birthmark
or skin scarred smooth
hidden beneath clothes
to surface on the wedding night

your body gave away so much of you
gave a way for hands
you wanted a tattoo –
with a pen
we drew the possibilities –
you stretched a leg towards the mirror
to see the paisley on your hip
i held another mirror behind you
the butterfly on your lower back

Calcutta

RAJINDERPAL S. PAL

we flew in
from separate continents
met on sudder street
in a hotel
where shashi kapoor and jennifer kendall
often stayed
or so the photographs
in the stairway
would have us believe

second/third generation servants
white gloved, waxed moustaches
feather fans on their turbans
serve Yorkshire puddings
        custard pies
to third/fourth generation imperialists
        "oh, the children
        the big brown eyes
        their dark hair –
        they are so lovely"

a jet-lagged first afternoon
we lay together as strangers
geckoes on the ceiling
bollywood song videos on the small television
the sound muted

we fell asleep
and awoke to the sound of a political rally
the amplified speech filling our room
    "the necessities –
    clean water
    safety on the streets
    basic education for our children"

as you measured drops of lavender oil
into the claw foot tub
we knew we had undressed too soon
and stood in the steam
unsure hands dangled awkwardly at our sides

in the tub we sat on opposite ends
and bathed each other like children
offering tired arms
to have them soaped and rinsed clean

if we could only recover
the promise of poems
and how i grew soft
once inside you

Rajinderpal S. Pal

~ *199*

Trust

RAJINDERPAL S. PAL

to fall here
you have to trust
the softness of snow
the enormity of sky

a winter morning in kananaskis
we walked a frozen river-bed
fresh snow over ice
under the ice flowing water
clear in the shade
green under sunlight

we stood still
our heavy boots silenced
listened to the soft trickle beneath
visible winter breath
the river's half hibernation

back at the hotel
so many layers
to unzip, unbutton, untie, unhook, unclasp, pull over
we collapsed
undone down our middles like cut fruit
bits of styrofoam –
that stippled ceiling –
snowed down on us
found the folds of our skins

Splendour

RAJINDERPAL S. PAL

and because we were unprepared
and because it was forbidden
we took shelter
from the street and the rain
in a concrete tunnel
in a school playground
where streetlights could not detect us

your hand reached back
angled my hardness to fit under

and when mouths and tongues could no longer continue
fingers pressed on vertebrae through cotton summer dress
your cheek hot against my shirt
your eyelash – a soft rhythm on my shoulder

we strive for fabric and texture
to relive the moment when for once
sense and senses
came together
we want some impossible permanence
not these arrivals and departures
not this ephemeral flutter

Contributors

ANITA AGRAWAL lives in Toronto. Her short story highlights the complexities that both liberal and conservative institutions impose on young South Asian women during the formation of their sexual identity.

AZIZA AHMED spent a year in South Africa "learning from women who sell sex for a living – learning lessons no one else can teach and inspiring thoughts only few can inspire. I want to help redefine how women operate in this secret world and make it real on paper, so no one can deny it."

SARA AHMED lives in Houston and is not nearly as promiscuous as she seems. In between working and procrastinating about graduate school, she envies Oscar Wilde's writings and tried to fight off her mid-twenties unsuccessfully.

NAVNEET ALANG was born in London, but is content in Toronto, while memories of a Punjab that no longer exist still happily cling to her. She is doing the academic thing. Her dream is to write the world's funniest joke book – because making people smile is what it's all about.

NEELANJANA BANERJEE is the managing editor of *Youth Outlook* magazine. The former editor-in-chief of *AsianWeek* newspaper, her writing has appeared in *Clamor*, *Hyphen*, *Audrey*, and the *Asian Pacific American Journal*.

KAREEMA BESH is a 26-year-old South Asian Yankee living (a double life) in New York City. Aside from writing, she enjoys frenzied Saturdays, lazy Sundays, and being a 2 on the Kinsey scale.

A character in an upcoming novel – thirty-six and single, MILAN BOSE is nursing a throbbing post-dot-com hangover, living in airport lounges and yoga retreats, avoiding four women, toxic parents, business-school debt, and making choices.

RASHMI CHOKSEY is a queer-identified woman living in Los Angeles. Her second, unpaid, but very rewarding job is as president of Trikone Los Angeles, a lesbian, gay, bisexual, transgender organization serving Southern California.

ROOHI CHOUDHRY is a writer, researcher, and incurable nomad, currently based in San Francisco. Her publications include *Hyphen Magazine* and *Bookslut.com*. She recently began work on her novel at a writing residency awarded by the Mesa Refuge.

SHOMPABALLI DATTA played, loved, struggled, resisted, grew up, and forged bonds in several cities in India. She continues to grow, learn, write, and love in Tuscaloosa, Alabama. She learns especially from her students at Stillman College.

RAYWAT DEONANDAN is an Indo-Guyanese Canadian presently living in Washington, D.C. His newest book, a novel titled *Divine Elemental*, will be published by TSAR Publications in 2003. Visit him online at *deonandan.com*.

TANUJA DESAI HIDIER's first novel *Born Confused* is both a Larry King and *Sunday Times* (London) book of the week, and ALA BBYA book of the year. She has also worked as a filmmaker and is lead singer/ songwriter in a band, currently recording a CD of original songs inspired by *Born Confused*. Her website is: *ThisIsTanuja.com*.

ANNIE DIJKSTRA learnt more about herself in Sri Lanka. This is her first published material. She thanks Dini and the Podi Menike. Homosexuality in Sri Lanka is still a crime carrying a potential prison sentence.

Contributors

MEHAROONA GHANI, born and raised in the Rocky Mountain town of Golden, British Columbia, now lives in Victoria. She encourages joining writing collectives. Her own have been a strong source of support in her own writing journey.

R. ISMAIL is a journalist for a newspaper, longing for a day when words will take her away from the job. She hopes to conquer her fears and write more poetry, fiction, and the like.

Soon after he stopped believing in reality, IGNATIUS J. met an undershirt that accused him of cowardice. Ignatius retorted that being a coward was still better than being a wife-beater.

SHARMEEN KHAN'S first name is derived from the Urdu word *sharum* which means shy and modest. Her hobbies are alternative radio, writing soft-core revolutionary porn for anti-racist publications, and making pakoras.

DR PRASENJIT MAITI'S work will be digitized at the Poetry Library at the South Bank Centre, London under a project funded by the Arts Council of England.

VIKAS MENON lives and writes in Brooklyn. His poems have appeared in *TriQuarterly*, *Toronto Review*, *APA Journal*, and *Monolid*, among others. He hopes to continue to expand his languages of intimacy.

KULJIT MITHRA lives in Markham, Ontario, with his lovely wife, Mandeep. His first published story "Silent Passengers" appeared in *Bolo! Bolo!*

SUNITA S. MUKHI is the author of *Doing the Desi Thing: Performing Indianess in New York City*. Her work has appeared in the anthologies *Contours of the Heart*, *A Patchwork Shawl*, and in the magazines *ArtSpiral* and *Little India*.

SUNIL NARAYAN, AKA fatty samosa & "your expletive of choice," born a child of the moon, is a one boi ABQD revolution. When not pontificating, dancing, or being a lush, he teaches kidz in hotlanta.

Journalist AMBER NASRULLA lives in Toronto. She has written for *The Globe and Mail, Chatelaine, The National Post,* and *Cottage Life* magazine. Most recently, she was CTV's Manager of Communications for News.

RAJINDERPAL S. PAL is the author of the *poetry collections pappaji wrote poetry in a language i cannot read* (TSAR) and *Pulse* (Arsenal Pulp), from which these poems appear. He lives in Calgary.

GILES PINTO was born in Pakistan but grew up mainly in Saudi Arabia, and he's currently working on a novel based on that experience. Now engaged, he lives in Toronto.

SANDIP ROY edits *Trikone Magazine* and has published in anthologies like *Contours of the Heart, Queer View Mirror, Quickies, Q&A, Men on Men 6, Mobile Cultures,* among others.

MEHNAZ SAHIBZADA was born in Pakistan and raised in California. She is currently working toward her PhD in Religion at UC Santa Barbara; she is also writing a novel entitled *Curry and Cacti.*

SALACIOUS SISTER is a queer, sex-positive activist who is right pissed-off at the need to use a pen-name due to the conservative nature of the South Asian community.

REENA SHARMA is a lifelong member of the FBI (Fiji-born Indians), a clandestine group existing in various pockets of the U.S. and Canada.

NAZNEEN SHEIKH is a Canadian novelist of Pakistani origins. She is the author of three adolescent novels and two works of adult fiction, and has written for the *The Globe and Mail, Toronto Star,* and *Now,* and has contributed to four anthologies.

SIDDARTH has been to known to astound many with his witty way with words and seductively sweet glances. He proclaims to know the secrets to what he calls "the white delight."

NAVJIT SINGH was born in Mexico, raised and educated across Asia, Africa, and Europe, and has had the benefit of a nomadic living, eclectic education, cosmopolitan upbringing, and a set of very supportive friends. He currently resides in Toronto.

NISHANT VAJPAYEE is currently working on a novel and a collection of four novellas that explore second-generation South Asian Americans' sexuality and reflect upon modern North American society. "Desi Families" is from the novel *Desi Lovin'*.

WANDERER lives in southern Ontario and likes sunshine, blue skies, and two-way conversations.

ASOKA WEERASINGHE is an award-winning poet, originally from Sri Lanka who has published 13 poetry books and chapbooks in England, Wales, U.S., Sweden, Sri Lanka, and Canada. He resides in Ottawa, Canada.

ZAR was born in Pakistan, migrated to Canada, and is currently pretending to study in Quebec, and one day hopes to become a world-class author, a nomadic wanderer, and a great ball of joy.

Desilicious

Editors

DEBORAH BARRETTO (right) was born in New Delhi, India and has lived most of her life in Toronto. She worked for Women's Press for six years where she learned about the world of publishing and met many inspiring women. She spends her working hours at MediaWatch. Deborah's passions are her son, Javed, flamenco dancing, and reading.

GURBIR SINGH JOLLY (centre) is currently at York University in Toronto, pursuing a PhD in postcolonial religious mysticism. He has taught various Canadian literature, cultural studies, and English composition courses. He loves his ma, his sister, and his dog. One day he hopes to teach very mysterious things based on Leonard Cohen's belief that there's a blaze of light in every word.

ZENIA WADHWANI (left) is a part-time PhD student in the Communication & Culture program at York University in Toronto, and a recent recipient of the Action Canada Fellowship. Much of her career has been spent working with youth, but her passions lie in the arts and culture scene and on issues pertaining to South Asia. She is an active volunteer, and one day, hopes to be a question on *Jeopardy!*.

PHOTO: JAG GUNDU

808.
3085   DESILICIOUS: SEXY,
DES   SUBVERSIVE, SOUTH
        ASIAN

$16.95

FINKELSTEIN
MEMORIAL LIBRARY
SPRING VALLEY, N.Y.

JAN 9 2007